Meet the  series and their brave K-9 partners

Officers: Cheyenne Chen and Jack Donadio

K-9 Partner: Beau the electronics-detecting chocolate Lab

Assignment: Protect tech analyst Cheyenne from lethal hitmen!

Officer: US Marshal Lorelai Danvers

K-9 Partner: Bixby the tracking-expert Australian shepherd

Assignment: Catch a threatening fugitive—and protect rancher Drake Corbin!

Lynette Eason is the bestselling, award-winning author with over three million copies sold. Lynette speaks and teaches at writing conferences all over the country when she's not writing and agenting. She lives in Greer, South Carolina, with her husband of almost thirty years. They have two grown children and a terribly spoiled American Eskimo pup. Lynette can be found online at www.lynetteeason.com, where you can sign up for her monthly newsletter, www.Facebook.com/lynette.eason and @lynetteeason on X.

Lenora Worth writes for Love Inspired and Love Inspired Suspense. She is a Carol Award finalist and a *New York Times*, *USA TODAY* and *Publishers Weekly* bestselling author. She writes Southern stories set in places she loves, such as Georgia, Texas, Louisiana and Florida. Lenora is married and has two grown children and now lives on a lake in the Panhandle of Florida. She loves reading, shoe shopping, long walks on the beach, mojitos and road trips.

CHRISTMAS K-9 PATROL

LYNETTE EASON
LENORA WORTH

If you purchased this book without a cover you should be aware that this book is stolen property. It was reported as "unsold and destroyed" to the publisher, and neither the author nor the publisher has received any payment for this "stripped book."

Special thanks and acknowledgment are given to Lynette Eason and Lenora Worth for their contributions to the Dakota K-9 Unit miniseries.

ISBN-13: 978-1-335-95739-9

Recycling programs for this product may not exist in your area.

Christmas K-9 Patrol

Copyright © 2025 by Harlequin Enterprises ULC

Deadly Christmas Trap
Copyright © 2025 by Harlequin Enterprises ULC

Dangerous Holiday Manhunt
Copyright © 2025 by Harlequin Enterprises ULC

All rights reserved. No part of this book may be used or reproduced in any manner whatsoever without written permission.

Without limiting the author's and publisher's exclusive rights, any unauthorized use of this publication to train generative artificial intelligence (AI) technologies is expressly prohibited.

This is a work of fiction. Names, characters, places and incidents are either the product of the author's imagination or are used fictitiously. Any resemblance to actual persons, living or dead, businesses, companies, events or locales is entirely coincidental.

For questions and comments about the quality of this book, please contact us at CustomerService@Harlequin.com.

® is a trademark of Harlequin Enterprises ULC.

Love Inspired
22 Adelaide St. West, 41st Floor
Toronto, Ontario M5H 4E3, Canada
www.LoveInspired.com

Printed in Lithuania

CONTENTS

DEADLY CHRISTMAS TRAP 7
Lynette Eason

DANGEROUS HOLIDAY MANHUNT 107
Lenora Worth

DEADLY CHRISTMAS TRAP

Lynette Eason

Dedicated to my amazing family. I love you most.

Have not I commanded thee? Be strong and of a good courage; be not afraid, neither be thou dismayed: for the Lord thy God is with thee whithersoever thou goest.
—*Joshua* 1:9

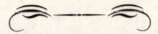

ONE

5:15 p.m.
Mid December
Plains City, South Dakota

Cheyenne Chen loved her job. But she loved her friends more, and was happy to leave the Plains City Police Department where she worked as a tech analyst. Although she'd been a cop for a few years, she was content to ride a desk these days. Still, she couldn't say she was sad to leave that desk behind for a few hours of fun and laughter with her friends as the holidays approached.

Assuming she could get there in one piece.

The person riding her bumper on the South Dakota highway was going to cause them both problems if he didn't back off. She tapped her brakes, but not too hard. Just to let him know she didn't appreciate his proximity.

He backed off a fraction. She let out a low breath and turned her attention back to the road—and her friends.

She was on her way to Daniel Slater's home. Daniel was the head of the Dakota Gun Task Force, which was created nine months ago to crack down on a dangerous weapons smuggling ring operating across North and South Dakota. Just recently, the guns had been recovered and the ringleader and the buyers had been brought to justice. As tech analyst for the task force, which operated out of the Plains City police station, Cheyenne had become close to her teammates. During their time together, they'd all become fast friends, and Daniel had invited everyone over for pizza, games and a present swap night at his home.

She was grateful for this group—surely one of them would let her spend Christmas with them this year. Her mother had texted and said not to come home to San Francisco, as her parents were going to China for two months to visit Uncle Wei.

Cheyenne had no idea who Uncle Wei was.

So, she'd stay here. And tonight, she'd let her need for a place to spend Christmas known. Maybe even spend it with Jack Donadio?

She really shouldn't get too excited about that idea, but she couldn't stop the thought from bouncing through her mind. Thinking about her coworker, with his stylishly messy brown hair, expressive green eyes and perpetual five o'clock shadow sent warm fuzzies all through her and her heart softened with the thought of being with him. The reaction annoyed her and thrilled her at the same time because while she was ready to find someone and settle down, dating Jack could completely upend her life. And that terrified her.

Living in Plains City, South Dakota, was a far cry from the small town near Silicon Valley where she'd grown up, but she'd made a life here and had "her people." It was more than she'd ever had before and not something she took for granted. Ever. Which was why being more than friends with Jack caused her to hesitate. Allowing something romantic to develop meant it had the chance to go wrong. And then where would she be? Without his friendship, the other friends who'd become her people—and the life she loved.

But she had to admit, before Jack had been shot in a raid gone wrong almost a year ago, they'd been growing closer while never crossing any lines to take their friendship further. And while that made her sad, it was also a self-protective thing as well. Growing up, she never felt like she measured up to those in her circle. Not with high school peers who'd driven to school in their Teslas, Bentleys and Lamborghinis.

Yes, her family had been comfortable, but definitely not lavish and she'd been made to feel "less than" by those who ridiculed her for not having every material thing they had.

She'd thought she'd overcome that, but when she was around Jack, for some reason that feeling surfaced. It was annoying and embarrassing. She sighed and checked her mirror again.

The driver was back and closer this time. If he was going to be that careless, why not just pass her and be done with it?

Snow had fallen over the past few days and the subzero temps could make driving treacherous and while the roads had been scraped, even with a tailgater, she took her time as there could still be patches of black ice. Sunset happened early this time of year with darkness falling around four fifteen and soon the lights from the urban streets gave way to a quieter, more rural area. In her mind's eye, she could picture the Black Hills in the distance to her right and the snow-covered fields on either side of the two-lane highway. Daniel didn't live far outside of the city limits, and she would be there in about ten minutes even at her slow crawl. Cheyenne stayed to the right, praying no one—

Lights from behind blinded her and she adjusted the rearview mirror to lessen the glare while she gently tapped her brakes yet again. The car behind her drew closer. And closer still. *What* was his problem?

And now he was so close she didn't know how he hadn't bumped her. If she dared press her brakes…

The hit to her bumper was hard and sent her spinning clockwise. She swallowed her scream and gripped the wheel trying to gain control, hit a patch of ice and skidded off the side of the road onto the shoulder, then shot out into the open grassy field. She bumped and rolled before hitting the brakes and jerking to a stop. A loud crash behind her pulled her out of her shocked stupor and she threw open the door.

The vehicle that had hit her was upside down. While she had

gone through an opening in the guardrails, the other car had hit one and flipped over it to land on its roof.

"Oh, no." She took a quick physical inventory and when nothing hurt, opened her door and stepped out. Her legs nearly buckled, but she held on to the doorframe until they steadied. Shock could do strange things to a person.

Thankfully, the snow on the ground wasn't deep and had stopped falling from the sky. She felt for her phone but couldn't find it. She had no time to search for it if the guy in the other vehicle needed immediate medical attention. She gathered her wits and ran to the overturned SUV.

The Chevy Tahoe was still, the engine running—and smoke coming from somewhere. Anger surged, but she stomped it down. The driver had been reckless with his driving and almost managed to kill both of them, but if she could help him, she would. Unless he *meant* to run her off the road? But why? One never knew these days. A woman alone in the dark on a road…

She looked back to see if anyone had stopped, but the accident had happened with no witnesses in sight. It was up to her. But if he had meant her harm, then she was walking right into danger. The driver let out a pained groan and she decided to risk it. He needed help. She approached the vehicle's side with caution and found him lying on the interior roof. Blood dripped from his head.

Either he hadn't been wearing his seat belt or he'd taken it off. "Are you okay?" she asked. Probably a dumb question.

"Can you help me out?" He sounded weak, his words slurred.

Cheyenne glanced in the direction of the road once more. Still no traffic. She didn't like the smoke coming from the car. She reached in. "You could have a head injury. I'm not sure you should move. If you give me your phone, I'll call 911."

"Just get me out. Please."

She bit her lip and reached through the window where glass had shattered and fallen away. "Grab my hand and I'll help pull you out. The window's broken, just crawl through it."

His hard fingers wrapped around hers and with minimal fuss, he was through the window. He lay on his back on the ground, breathing hard, eyes closed. She couldn't see the color in his face well, but thought he looked a little gray. "You hit your head."

"Yeah."

"Hold on and I'll get help here."

"No." He rolled to his feet and swayed, then grabbed her wrist. He might be unsteady on his feet, but his grip was strong enough.

A flash of fear shot through her. "What are you doing?"

"Where's your car?"

"Over there, in the field you knocked it into." She tried to jerk free and he held on. Another fissure of alarm shimmied through her. She could get away from him by using her training, but he was hurt and she didn't want to add to it. "Why?"

"Because you're coming with me."

"No, I'm not. Let me go!" Adding to his injuries wasn't a concern any longer.

She kicked out, but he deflected the move and jerked her arms behind her back. Pain arched through her shoulders. She twisted, but even wounded he was strong. He moved her slight frame in the direction of her vehicle. In less than a second, she mentally flipped through the best self-defense moves, chose one and planted her feet, sending him off balance. He lost his grip on her right arm and she swung it around to connect her elbow with the side of his head. He cried out and stumbled back. Then landed on his rear end.

"Hey!" someone shouted from the road. His high beams illuminated the area. "Are you all right?"

"No! Call 911! Help!"

The man on the ground rolled to his feet and staggered toward her. He didn't look like he had much strength left, but apparently wasn't giving up.

"Why are you doing this?" She backed away from him, but

the slick snow, turning to ice in the subzero temperatures, caused her to skid while her feet scrambled for traction.

He lunged at her and missed. He went down again, but his hard hand clamped around her ankle, pulling her to the ground with him. She grunted at the hit and pain raced up her left hip. She ignored it and used her free foot to send a heel smashing into his nose. He howled and dropped back to the ground. "Stop it!" She couldn't help the shout. "Tell me why you're doing this!" She rolled to her feet and looked down at him.

Still, he made the effort to stand. "You're my payout. The bounty. I need the money."

"Bounty? What money?" He didn't answer, just stood, swaying. The need for information overruled her fear of him, especially because she assumed the person who'd stopped had called 911. She walked up to him and jabbed a finger in his chest. "What money?"

"Hey," a voice called, "I've got some medical training. Need some help?"

"I can help, too," another voice said.

They started her way and her would-be captor collapsed to the ground, eyes closed.

The two reached her. "Let me check him out," the first one said. "I'm Brian, by the way."

"Cheyenne."

"And I'm Hank," the second man offered. "I've called an ambulance. Should be here in a few minutes. Hopefully. Who knows with this weather?" He shot a concerned glance at Cheyenne. "Was he trying to force you to go with him?"

"Yes."

"Who is he?"

"No idea." She dropped beside the man who'd gone unconscious. The cold hit her all at once and she shivered, recognizing that even more shock was probably setting in. The faint sound of her phone ringing from the depths of her vehicle reached her and she figured it was most likely Jack or one of the others calling to ask where she was.

Brian worked on her would-be attacker, checking his pulse, his breathing, his eyes. He pulled the man's shirt apart and sucked in a breath. He looked up at her and Hank and shook his head. "If the bruising is any indication, he's got some massive internal bleeding. If they don't get here fast, he's not going to make it. I can't do anything without the proper tools."

"Does he have a wallet on him? The least we can do is see if we can find his next of kin and get them here while he's still alive. Let them know what happened and they can find him at the hospital. Maybe he lives close by." She thought about what he'd said. A bounty? Maybe he'd just been talking out of his head because of the severity of his injuries. Hallucinating? It was possible.

Hank patted the guy's pockets, found the stuffed wallet and tossed it to her.

Sirens finally sounded in the distance. "Thank you, Lord," she whispered.

She searched for a driver's license. It wasn't in the little plastic slot so she finally just pulled everything out. Two credit cards with the name Jeremy Kelley. Several grocery store coupons, a folded picture of a stick figure family and a printed picture of a phone number and—*her*?

K-9 officer Jack Donadio sat in the recliner in Daniel's den, sipping on a fresh Coke, watching the door, and scratching his K-9 Beau's silky ears.

Where was Cheyenne?

Beau whined and settled his snout on Jack's knee, encouraging his handler to continue the doggy massage. Jack smiled. Beau was trained to locate hidden electronic devices such as USB drives, SD cards and burner phones. Partnering with Beau had become a dream come true as Jack had been fascinated with this type of dog since he'd heard they could do such a thing. In his opinion, they were the perfect match thanks to Jack's expertise in all things related to busting technology-savvy bad guys.

But it was almost Christmas and time to have some fun celebrating the season. Jack kept a close eye on the door, ignoring the mistletoe hanging from it. Cheyenne should have been here by now and he was seriously getting concerned. He pictured the dark-haired, dark-eyed woman that he'd grown to care deeply for. They were friends. Good friends. But since he'd been injured, a distance had come between them. A greater distance than had been there previously and that was his fault.

He'd pulled away from her because of the uncertainty surrounding the injury he'd sustained in a shooting. It was something he'd not shared with anyone. Something that could cause him to lose his leg. The surgeons had left the bullet in his leg thanks to its location near the femoral artery. Right now, it was lodged in and only caused him pain when he moved a certain way. Most of the time he could forget it was there, but if the bullet shifted…

Yeah, not good. And he still didn't know who shot him. Part of him wondered if he'd ever find the person. He couldn't think about it too long or it darkened his mindset. And tonight, he just wanted to enjoy the friendships that surrounded him.

And Cheyenne.

He looked at the clock once more. Two minutes past the last time he'd looked. He was worried she was this late without calling to let one of them know why. He set his drink on the coaster and called her number for the third time. And for the third time, it rang to voicemail.

"Ugh."

"Everything okay?" Raina Graves asked. Raina was wife to Kenyon Graves, another member of the DGTF. She walked over to the Christmas tree in the corner of the room, straightened one of the ornaments and frowned at him.

"Cheyenne hasn't shown up yet and I've called her phone three times. No answer."

Her frown deepened. "That's weird."

"I know."

Daniel came in from the kitchen. "What's weird?"

He was going to have to call a meeting so he didn't have to keep repeating himself. "Cheyenne's not here and she's not answering—" His ringing phone cut him off. Cheyenne. "That's her. Hang on." He swiped the screen. "Hey, are you okay?"

"Yes, I'm okay, I've been in a wreck, but I'm not hurt. Just a few bumps and bruises. And one cut on my arm."

"A wreck?" He walked toward the front door and grabbed his coat from the coat rack. By now, several others from the team, Kenyon, husband and wife Zach and Eden Kelcey, and Lucy Lopez all frowned in unison at him. "I'm on my way," he said.

"Really, I'm okay. I'm just heading to the hospital to get checked out. I'll be fine."

"Right. See you there."

He hung up on her sputtering and looked at the others moving to grab their winter gear. "We can't all show up. I'll go and keep you updated." He made a clicking sound to bring Beau to his side and the dog hopped up, ready to do whatever Jack needed.

Raina looked like she might protest, but he grabbed his coat and headed out the door with Beau on his heels. The others could follow or not. He wasn't wasting any more time. He thought he heard Raina ask, "Why does he get to go?"

Understandable question. It wasn't like he and Cheyenne were a "thing," but his first instinct was to go to her. So that's what he would do.

Forty minutes later, he and Beau walked through the glass hospital doors and made his way to the emergency department. Even though he was out of uniform, Beau's vest identified him as a working dog. With a flash of Jack's badge, the ER nurse opened the double doors that led back to the rooms where patients were held. "She's in four."

"Thank you."

"Of course."

He knocked on the wall next to the pulled curtain. "It's me, Jack."

"Come in, but only if you're going to break me out of here."

Cheyenne's grumpy words turned his lips up with relief. He peered around the curtain and motioned Beau inside. The dog walked in and raised up on his hind legs to peer at Cheyenne. Her scowl faded and she reached out to scratch the dog's ears. "Hey, Beau buddy, glad to see you." Beau licked her hand and tried to sidle closer.

"How about me?" Jack asked.

"Always."

She smiled and he nodded to the bandage on her arm. Her long-sleeved shirt and had been cut away. "You okay?"

"I am, but the driver of the car who hit me isn't. He died at the scene."

"I'm sorry."

"I am, too. Mostly because I have questions." She bit her lip. "Jack, he deliberately ran me off the road and when I tried to help him, he grabbed me and was going to kidnap me. Obviously, it didn't go down how he planned, but it was a deliberate thing."

He blinked, trying to process the fact that she'd been in that kind of danger. "What? Why? Did he say?"

She slid off the bed and walked over to grab a pair of gloves from the box on the wall. "I need to show you something."

"Okay."

Jack watched, confused, but stayed silent while she pulled a piece of paper from her pocket. "I found this picture of me with a phone number in his wallet," she said. "I handled it without gloves before I realized what it was, but it definitely belonged to him, so his prints are most likely on it. I just don't know if anyone else's are. There was no driver's license. And if the credit cards found in his wallet don't belong to him, then maybe prints will tell us who he is."

Jack pulled on his own pair of gloves and took the picture with a frown. "He had this on him?"

She nodded. "And he said he couldn't let me go because he needed the money."

"What money?"

"That's what I asked. He said something about a bounty and then passed out."

He looked at the picture once more. A picture and a phone number. The amount of $250K had been written above her head. "Someone put a hit on you?"

"I don't have any idea." She pointed. "Maybe call that number and see what happens?"

"You didn't try it?"

She shook her head and flushed. "I almost did, I'll admit it, but I decided I wanted witnesses. Who knows who the number belongs to?"

"I've seen a lot in my years with law enforcement, but this is a new one." He shook his head, his heart squeezing at the thought of something happening to Cheyenne. "Why would there be a bounty on your head? Did he say?"

She shrugged. "He just said that he needed the money."

"But again, why *you*? Who's going to pay this bounty?"

"That's the question of the hour, isn't it?"

He looked from the paper back to her and then the paper once again, sure he'd misread or misunderstood. But he hadn't. What had she managed to get herself involved in? "Can you think of anyone you might have made mad lately?"

"No, of course not. At least not one specific person. If you count all the criminals I've helped put away with DGTF and the PCPD, then I guess it's a long list. Even if I'm behind the scenes."

He rubbed his forehead. "This is…"

"Yes, it is."

"Okay, we need a plan."

"Like what?"

"We kidnap you and turn you over to the person who wants you."

TWO

Cheyenne blinked. "Sure. Let's do that."

He quirked a smile at her. "Not really."

"I figured. But you're thinking something."

"Well, that was my first thought, but I'm not sure how we can make it work and keep you safe. It would take some investigating for the best way to do that. I suppose the first step would be to pull some of the DGTF together and see if they—and their supervisors—are willing to loan them out once more. If Cheyenne really has a bounty on her head, depending on how it was advertised, it's possible people are going to be coming from every location. With the DGTF's broad reach across multiple jurisdictions, it makes sense that we'll need a bigger network to figure this out than just local. We'll let the PCPD know what's going on, of course, but if we can lure the person out to meet one of us at whatever location he gives us, then we can get him and find out what this is all about."

"Sounds easy enough." It did. And that scared her. Because nothing was ever easy for her. "I'd have to be there, though. He'd probably want to see me."

"Yeah, that's the problem." He frowned.

"Hey, I can handle it if that's the route we need to go. I was a cop, remember? I'm trained."

"I know you are, but there are so many things that could go wrong—" He stopped. "Let me keep thinking. I'll discuss it with the others. In the meantime, I think we should put someone on your house. Make sure you have protection because if the guy who came after you had that information on you, it's possible other people could, too."

She flinched. Well, that was kind of terrifying. "All right, but can you call the number and see what happens?"

He hesitated, then shrugged and dialed. "The number you have dialed is no longer in service. Please check the number and try again."

"Okay. Weird. Why have a number that doesn't work on the ad?"

"I don't know." He frowned.

The nurse came in and walked Cheyenne through how to clean her wound and then executed her discharge. Jack stepped out of the room, phone to his ear, while the woman talked. When the nurse finished, she said, "I'll be back in a few minutes with your copies of the papers you just signed."

She exited and Jack reentered to look at Cheyenne. "Backup is on the way."

"Backup?"

"Someone to follow us back to your place. Unless you feel like going to Daniel's instead?"

"No. I don't think I'm up for socializing right now so good call."

"Okay. Jenna's off duty for the next couple of days so she and Augie are going to stay with you tonight if you're okay with that." A Cold River sheriff's deputy, Jenna had been a trusted member of the DGTF and Augie was her beautiful German shepherd trained in suspect apprehension.

"Well, if someone tries to grab me, Augie will make them sorry about that."

"Exactly, but hopefully police presence will be a deterrent until we can get our plan in place."

"Won't the police presence clue him in?"

He frowned. "Hmm...well, whoever is after you has probably done his homework. Knows you work with a bunch of cops. Maybe even knows you *were* a cop once upon a time. We'll keep it subtle and make it look like we're just concerned for a fellow coworker who was in a car accident. There's no way for anyone to know that even *you* know there's a possible bounty on your head. At least I don't think so, but it's a chance we have to take."

Okay, that was true.

Once she was in Jack's vehicle with Beau in his special area in the back, the shakes set in. She laced her fingers together to stop the trembling.

A warm hand covered hers and she jerked her gaze up to meet Jack's compassionate gaze. "It's going to be okay, Cheyenne."

She nodded and swallowed hard. Having Jack on her side meant the world to her. She circled back to the dilemma her attraction to him created. His friends were her friends, true enough, but they'd been his friends first, so... If they started seeing one another, then broke up...would she lose the people who'd become her family? Part of her desperately wanted their friendship to morph into something more—and before he'd been shot, he'd been pretty clear he was open to that. Then the shooting and during his recovery, she'd tried to be there for him and he'd been distant, keeping her at arm's length. It hurt, but it also drove home her fear that while she was crazy about him, if they ever did get together, it might blow up her life.

Tears pricked at her eyes at the thought. But for now, the future could wait. She would take solace in his presence and live in the moment. The future would be there to worry about later.

Four hours after the incident, he pulled into the driveway of her three-story townhome and parked in her spot. She sucked in a steadying breath and let it out slowly. He looked over at her. "You want me to arrange for a rental?"

"I'll do it. Thanks."

He rubbed a hand down his chin. "Jenna and Augie will be staying with you for a shift, then Beau and I'll be back for the rest of the night. I'd take first shift, but I...didn't sleep much the night before and it'd be better if I had a few hours of sleep before having to be alert."

Why hadn't he slept? Cheyenne sighed. It wasn't her business. "I'm sorry to be so much trouble. Don't you think my alarm system and my own weapon will be sufficient?" Once a cop, always a cop. If not by job description, definitely by mentality. She'd always have a weapon close by.

He shook his head. "I'd rather not risk someone slipping past that. And while I'm glad you have the weapon, I'd hate to see you have to use it."

"That's what I have it for." *Of course* she didn't want to shoot anyone if it could be avoided, but having her friends disrupt their schedules and their lives, missing sleep, because of her, rubbed her the wrong way. She'd been taking care of herself for a long time now.

"I know." He hesitated. "Let us help you, Cheyenne. Please. We *need* to help you. For our own peace of mind. What if it was one of us and we needed your help? How would you feel if that help was refused?"

She swallowed and gave a slow nod. "Okay, you've made your point. I'll do what you think is best."

"Good. Now, let me clear the place so you can get inside and get settled for the night."

She let him usher her into her own home and together they cleared the place. Empty. Nothing disturbed. All was well. She went to the kitchen. She needed something to do with her hands while she thought about everything. After fixing coffee, she threw together a small snack of cheese and crackers and fruit. It wasn't much, but she hadn't been to the store in a while so it would have to do. Jack joined her at the counter. "Don't think you can sleep just yet?"

"Not just yet."

He nodded and snagged a cracker. He plopped a piece of cheese on it and downed it. He was hungry and she wished she had a steak for him.

"Jenna will be here shortly and I'll leave you alone," he said.

"Thanks." She stopped. "That didn't come out right. I wasn't thanking you for leaving me alone, but thanks for...well, everything, I guess."

He smiled. "You're welcome." He popped another cracker and some cheese in his mouth. "So, we've had lots of chats about stuff, but I don't think you've ever told me what got you so interested in the tech world. Fill me in."

"Hmm. I've never told you that story?"

"Nope."

Probably not as she didn't volunteer the information that often. But she'd tell him tonight, thankful for the distraction. And it was time to start being open with him. "My parents were immigrants who landed in San Francisco. My dad had always wanted his own company so he and my mom started a small convenience store that was very successful. I used to help out there after school and during summer vacations." Always working. Feeling alone and left out of the fun her classmates seemed to have whenever they weren't in school. In hindsight, she was sure there were others who had to do the same as she, but she'd never noticed. She'd been too focused on her own loneliness.

"That's where you learned your work ethic."

She nodded, shrugging of the melancholy thoughts. God had brought great people into her life and she'd be thankful. "They're both incredibly hard workers, but the struggle was real in the beginning. We're not particularly close. I don't think they ever planned to have children. Their work was everything to them and that left little for fun or just being a family. And while I was resentful—and still am a little, I suppose—I can still admire them. They never quit, you know?"

"Admirable and sad all at the same time." His eyes were tender and she wasn't sure what to do with that.

She cleared her throat. "I'm sure it's because they came from nothing. Born in a poor area of China, they were determined to have a better life. And they did."

"But they sacrificed so much. They sacrificed a relationship with you."

"Yes, well, maybe one day they'll see that, but for now, our relationship works for us. I see them on holidays and touch base occasionally and they keep me in the will." She laughed, then sobered. "I guess that's not funny."

"Not really."

"I will say this. Watching them, I knew I didn't want that life. I want to be a good mom to the kids I'll have one day. I want to be present and make sure they feel wanted and know without a doubt that they're loved. So, at least I know what I want in that sense thanks to how I grew up."

"Your kids will be blessed to have you for a mom."

Heat started to crawl into her cheeks and she needed to change the subject before she did something stupid like lean over and kiss him. "All that to say, I wanted to make a difference in the world so I started searching to figure what that looked like. It happened my sophomore year in college. I was studying computer science at Berkley because I knew that I was gifted with the ability to excel in that area." She shrugged. "But I was still searching for my purpose here. One of my roommates was from the area and I started going to her church. Got really involved in the community. God eventually led me to volunteer at a women's shelter on the weekends and the holidays I didn't go home. I met this one person who was running from shelter to shelter because her ex was stalking her. He'd stolen her identity and wiped out their savings, posted horrible things on her social media as her which caused her to lose her kids and so on."

"That's awful."

"I know what it's like to be a victim—and before you ask, think high school bully and a group of mean girls—so it made me very angry on her behalf when she told me about it. I worked to turn all of that around for her. I found him and did a little stalking of my own. I watched everything he did online and caught him in the stalking, found proof that he'd hacked her accounts, found all the threatening messages that he sent her and deleted—including ones that taunted her about taking her kids away from her—and so on. I took it all and turned it over to the local police for her. Two months later, she had her kids back and he was up on charges. Last I heard, she was living with her sister and putting her life back together."

"That's amazing, Cheyenne."

She smiled. "Thanks. I felt amazing for sure to help her like that. It was then I realized I wanted to do that for my job. I joined the police force and worked my way up through the ranks and I guess my tech skills caught the attention of the PCPD. The rest, they say, is history." There was more, but no need to go into that now.

He shook his head. "I can't believe I never asked you about that."

"It's okay. I don't talk about it much."

"Why not?"

She shrugged. "I just don't. There are better things to talk about than my past."

He paused. "Wait a minute. You said you knew what it felt like to be a victim? A victim of what?"

She froze. She'd said that? "It's not important." There were things in her past she'd rather forget. Telling Jack about them required a vulnerability she wasn't sure she could find as it might cause him to think less of her. Or worse, pity her. "All that matters is I overcame it and love where I am in life now and will protect it with everything in me."

He nodded, but she could see the questions in his eyes.

He wasn't going to let it go. So now she had to figure out how to avoid the questions when they came.

Great.

She left him in the kitchen, his eyes shooting his curiosity into an invisible target on her back. Then he moved to the nearest window to peer out and she was reminded that someone had put a real target there. With that soul-shuddering thought, she walked into her bedroom and shut the door. Then checked the window to make sure it was locked. And under the bed to make sure her imaginary childhood monsters hadn't returned.

Then again, who had time to worry about those when a real-life monster appeared to be after her?

After telling him more about her background, Cheyenne had bid him good-night and disappeared. He had a feeling she'd just touched the surface of her growing-up years, but was glad to get to know her a little better—even if she was holding something back from him.

Which wasn't surprising.

They'd been friends for a while, but not true, share-your-soul friends. They'd only scratched the surface of who they were with one another, each of them unwilling to pull down their respective walls very far. Before the shooting, he'd just been trying to tread carefully with Cheyenne, not push her too hard or too fast, letting her set the pace. Then after the shooting and his recovery, thinking everything was going to be fine, the doctor dropped his medical bomb on Jack. And Jack had taken a step back, uncertainty about everything causing him to put romance on the back burner even while their friendship flourished.

But now?

He was getting tired of letting fear rule his life.

His reaction to Cheyenne's call for help shocked him. The sheer panic that had raced through him leaving him almost shaking definitely opened his eyes to the fact that he wanted to be there for her, to comfort her. Be the one she turned to—in addition to the other friends in their lives who dropped everything to help someone in trouble. Especially when it was one of their team.

As soon as he let them know what was going on, his phone blew up with offers of help—at least from those who were still in the area and hadn't been at Daniel's house to get the news firsthand. They all were a part of the task force unit that had been formed from multiple agencies. As they'd worked together over the past months, they'd formed strong bonds of friendship. Lifetime bonds.

And now, hours later, it was his and Beau's turn to take a shift to watch Cheyenne's home. She had an end unit townhome in one of the nicer areas of the city and all was quiet this time of night.

Jenna and Augie walked over to him and he rolled his window down. Beau stuck his head out for a scratch and Jenna obliged.

"You get some sleep?" she asked him.

"I did. A desperately needed five consecutive hours."

"And yet, you were going to be at game night," she said, raising a brow. The calculating glint in her eyes made him want to squirm.

He refused. "We never have enough time to get together and just hang out with all of us from different places. I wasn't about to miss out."

"That's valid. I just thought Cheyenne's presence might have prompted you to be there."

"Cute."

"And not wrong. When are you going to ask her out?" Jenna was engaged to rancher Clay Miller and planning a wedding so it wasn't surprising she was trying her hand at matchmaking...

"I plead the fifth." He was beginning to regret all the times he'd offered his own unsolicited advice to his friends. It was definitely coming around full circle.

"You do that. In the meantime, it's my turn to grab some sleep. Call if you need anything."

"Will do. Thanks again."

Jenna left and Beau rested his snout on Jack's shoulder. "Guess it's just you and me, boy," he said to the dog and gave his heavy head a rub. Beau licked his ear in thanks and Jack smiled, then shifted to reach for his thermos of coffee on the passenger seat. An arc of pain raced up his leg and back and he froze, moved more gently this time while the pain faded.

Fabulous. Getting shot wasn't just a one and done and move

on with life. Nope. He still had a bullet inside him that was a constant reminder. Thankfully, it didn't slow him down much and he'd passed all the physical requirements to return to duty, but every so often if he twisted just so…

Yeah, better to not do that.

He grabbed his phone and checked his own case file. "Assailant unknown. Still at large." He had no idea who shot him and most likely, he never would. Somehow he was going to have to figure out a way to be at peace with that.

Movement from the corner of Cheyenne's house caught his attention and he straightened, grateful for the absence of any pain with that motion. Jack opened the door and climbed out, keeping his gaze on the area where he'd seen…something.

Beau jumped out to stand beside him, body quivering, sensing he might be getting ready to work. "Beau, heel." Jack walked forward, hand on his weapon, eyes searching the darkness while Beau stayed right at his side. A walk around the perimeter turned up nothing, but the trees that lined the back of the townhome community concerned him. They'd be an excellent hiding place for someone to keep watch. He and Beau walked toward them and Beau's nose was on high alert even though he had no order to search.

He rounded the corner of Cheyenne's house and everything looked fine. Except…

One of the window screens had been slashed and the window was open.

THREE

Cheyenne lay still, eyes wide in the dark room. Something had jerked her awake. The alarm was silent, but her floor creaked. She turned her head toward the window. The silhouette of a man just inside almost pulled a scream from her. She didn't move, didn't breathe, just watched him take a step toward her, then stop. Almost as though he was trying to make up his mind about what to do.

He walked toward her bed. She could make out his ski mask now that he'd moved into the beam of the moonlight filtering through the window he'd just climbed in. Panic clawed at her, but she refused to move.

Think!

"You're awake, aren't you?" he asked, his voice low and pleasant. As though they were discussing the weather or the most recent movie they'd just seen. "I was hoping you wouldn't wake up just yet. Guess I have to go with plan B." He pulled a rope from his back pocket.

In one continuous movement, Cheyenne grabbed her weapon from the end table where she'd placed it last night and rolled to the other side of the bed, then onto the floor, dragging the covers with her. She rose to her knees, and aimed her gun, arms resting on her mattress.

"Get out or I'll shoot!"

Her yell gave him pause, but then he turned and dove back

out the window. She heard the thud on the other side and a dog barked. Beau or Augie? Cheyenne kicked away the sheets and blankets and raced to the window on bare feet to see the intruder running down the street.

Jack and Beau took off after him. "Police! Stop!"

But the guy kept going. She slammed the window shut and found a hole in her glass. So that's how he'd managed to unlock the window. A simple glass cutter. She darted to the front of the house and threw open the front door to see Jack and Beau still chasing the guy.

"I said stop! Or I'll release the dog." Jack's ferocious yell did the trick. The suspect had no way of knowing the chocolate Lab specialized in electronics detection, not suspect apprehension.

The guy froze, then shot his hands in the air. Jack got on the radio and requested backup. Then said, "Get on your knees and lock your fingers behind your head."

Cheyenne darted down the steps and inched close enough to hear what was going on. The intruder hesitated and turned and she thought he might do as ordered, but then he bolted. Because he didn't think a Lab would chomp as hard as a German shepherd?

Jack and Beau, who liked a good chase like any other dog, ran after him. The man darted back toward the front of the townhouse. His feet pounded the asphalt, and Beau shot forward.

The guy kept going, but glanced back and saw Beau right on his heels. Cheyenne continued right behind them all, ignoring the fact that her feet were just about frozen.

"Beau! Attack!"

Cheyenne almost laughed. Beau had no idea what that word meant, but the fleeing guy didn't know that.

Jack's strategy worked. The guy looked back once more and in the glow of the streetlight, Cheyenne saw his eyes go wide and then he stumbled to a stop in the middle of the road. He went to his knees and slapped his hands against the back of his head and laced his fingers together. "I'm down, I'm down! Don't let him bite me!"

"Beau, heel." The dog trotted over to Jack and watched him with expectant eyes. Jack patted his head. "Good boy." He approached the man who stayed still as a statue. "Hands behind your back. You're under arrest for attempted burglary."

Cheyenne stood watching while Jack and Beau walked the handcuffed man down her street toward his official SUV parked on her curb. She shivered when a cold wind whipped her hair around her face. And she stomped her numb feet. She needed to get them warm, but she hated to leave just yet.

Pushing aside the strands, she simply waited until Jack noticed her. His tight jaw loosened a fraction. "Hold on a sec. Let me get him secured." Sirens sounded and he glanced at her. "I called for backup when I saw the screen had been cut."

She nodded.

Two other officers she recognized hurried toward them. Jack shoved the prisoner at the nearest one. "Can you transport this one for me? I've got questions for him."

"Sure thing."

Once the prisoner was secured in the back of the officer's vehicle, he and Beau approached her. "Jenna left and it wasn't five minutes after she was gone that I noticed that guy and went after him," Jack said. "I saw the screen had been cut and your window open. It wasn't your bedroom, but the one next to it."

She nodded and shivered, rubbing her arms. "Yeah, I saw that too. That's the guest room. He cut a hole in the glass so I'm guessing that's how he got the window unlocked, climbed in then came to find me. So what does he want?"

"I haven't had a chance to talk to him, but I'm going to say he's after you."

"For the two hundred fifty grand payout."

"Yeah." He looked down. "Cheyenne! Your feet." He hustled her inside and hurried her to the bathroom. "Run warm water before you wind up losing toes."

"I know. That was dumb." What had she thought she could do in her bare feet? In the freezing cold?

She sighed and wiggled her toes. "They all work. I'll soak them for a few minutes, then change and follow you to the station. I want to observe the interrogation."

"I'll wait. I'll call ahead and let them know we're coming."

"Works for me."

She did as promised, soaking her feet, and nothing seemed damaged. *Thank you, God. That was a little stupid.* She could picture him nodding in agreement. She was ready within ten minutes and walked outside to find Jack leaning against the car. "I'll follow you if that's okay," she said.

"I'd rather you ride with me. You've already had two people after you. I don't want you in the car alone."

He might be right. She grabbed her purse and climbed into the passenger seat. "You knew I'd want to go, didn't you?" she asked once he and Beau were settled.

"Figured you'd insist on it."

"That's why you asked for him to be transported in another vehicle. So I wouldn't have to ride with him."

He shot her a quick smile and wheeled the vehicle toward the station. "Exactly."

"I appreciate it." He was thoughtful and caring and good-looking and smart and…yeah, all of those things and more. So many reasons why her heart belonged to him. Not that she'd intentionally let that happen, but…yeah. It was also a heart he hadn't indicated he wanted lately. Which saddened her when it should have relieved her. Her wishy-washiness was about to send her over the edge. She wanted Jack with everything in her, but she just couldn't get past the fear that if she risked it and lost him, she'd lose everything.

She tossed off those thoughts and stayed quiet the rest of the drive to the Plains City Police Department. It was early morning and she hadn't slept well to begin with, but she ignored the fatigue and followed Jack and Beau into the station and down the hall to the interrogation room.

Jack waved her into the room with the two-way mirror where she'd watch. "You okay?"

She nodded. "I'm okay." Or she would be.

"Beau can keep you company."

"I'd love that."

Jack commanded the dog to stay with her and Beau seemed happy to oblige. Jack left the room and she settled into the nearest chair with Beau on the floor at her side. Seconds later, Jack entered the interrogation room and the prisoner looked up. Shortly after that, Detective West Cole walked in, too. Cheyenne raised a brow. Jack must have called him when she'd been changing clothes. West had been part of the task force when they'd been working to take down a gun ring, but the two men had been friends before that since they worked out of the same department.

Captain Douglas Ross, Jack and West's boss, stepped inside as well and shut the door. The prisoner eyed the three men in front of him and linked his fingers together on the table.

"Let's start with your name," Jack said.

The man hesitated, then sighed. "Carter Pullman."

"All right, Mr. Pullman," West said, "Why did you break into Ms. Chen's home?"

"I didn't. Exactly. I mean—"

Jack snorted. "You're really going to go that route?"

The man sighed and lifted his bound hands to press them against his eyes. "Okay, so I did get in. But I wasn't going to hurt her. I just needed to…borrow her."

"Borrow me?" Cheyenne muttered. "That's a new one."

"Tell us everything," Jack said, "and we'll let the DA know you cooperated."

For a moment, Pullman stared at his hands. Then looked up with a sigh. "I need money," he said. "I'm about to lose everything. I was let go from my job about eight months ago and I haven't been able to find anything that pays all the bills. I have a wife and three kids."

"Go on," Jack said.

"About two weeks ago, I was looking online for anything that paid—and paid fast—and ventured into the dark web." He shook his head. "I know the dark web isn't all bad, but you can definitely find things on there that aren't on Google. Honestly, I just needed something paid and as long as it didn't break the law, I was willing to do it."

Jack raised a brow. "Last I looked, kidnapping is breaking the law."

"But bounty hunters aren't held to the same laws as ordinary citizens," Pullman said. Cheyenne grimaced. That was true. "I mean I wasn't specifically looking for a bounty hunter job, but one of my search requests must have triggered one of the keywords or something and there it was. Her picture with the two hundred fifty K bounty."

"It said bounty. It used that word?"

"Yes. The ad was a call for bounty hunters and the first payoff was Cheyenne Chen. It said she'd skipped bail and if she was brought in, it would be a major payday. Not everything on the dark web is dark. It looked legit. And like I said, bounty hunting is legal, so I decided to go for it."

Right, but *legal* didn't mean safe. There'd already been two attacks on Cheyenne. How many more were coming?

Jack's hands curled into fists and he had to make the conscious effort to release them. "The different phone numbers and only one chance to call? That didn't clue you in?"

Pullman bit his lip. "Yeah, it did, but it was too much money not to try."

"So you thought you'd go for it," West said.

"Yeah, I mean, as long as it's not illegal—"

"Breaking and entering is definitely illegal," Jack said. "Attempted kidnapping? Dude, you're facing all kinds of charges.

Charges that were witnessed by *two* law enforcement officers. Let that sink in for a moment. Your intended target works for the very police department you're in right now."

The man flushed. "I was just trying to see if she was home, that's all."

Jack smothered a huff. Sure he was. "Right. By climbing in her window."

"Bounty hunters can enter someone's home and use reasonable force to capture them. You know that as well as I do."

"And you're a certified bounty hunter?" West asked. "You've done the training?"

"Uh..." He sighed. "No, but the ad didn't say you had to be certified."

"But you do to enter someone's home and call yourself a bounty hunter," Jack said. "Without that certification, you're just another criminal."

The guy flushed and snapped his lips shut. Jack's head began to throb with a stupidity-induced headache. "Let's move past that for the moment. You needed to climb through her window to see if she was home because knocking on the door is no longer a thing or...?" He spread his hands in a silent question. He caught the captain's look and shot the man a nonverbal apology. He'd tone down the sarcasm.

"I noticed her windows weren't wired for the alarm system, but her doors were. So if she ran out the door or something, she'd set the alarm off and I'd lose my chance. I was going to hide, then wait until morning when she turned off the alarm and see if I could get her to come with me. If not, then I planned to persuade her it would be in her best interest to do so. That's all."

"And by persuade, you mean force her to go with you so you could deliver her to this unidentified place and collect the bounty."

"Well...yes." He frowned. "It sounds so wrong when you say it like that."

Jack refrained from face-palming and groaning. "Because it

is wrong," he said between clenched teeth. He made an effort to relax his jaw. "All that aside, is this the same flyer you saw on the dark web?"

He showed Pullman the one Cheyenne had taken off the dead guy. Pullman frowned. "It's close. It doesn't have all the information you can get by going to the web page, but that's the gist of it. Oh, and the phone number is different."

They'd have to get on the dark web and find out for themselves. "We called this number and it says it's disconnected," Ross said.

"From what I understand, it generates a different number with each printing. You put your information in the form and hit print. Each time it prints, you get a different number. And you can only put your information in once. That part's not on there. It's on the website. You call the number that you're given only when you have her. If you call and don't have her to bring in, you lose your shot. The number is obsolete as soon as you hang up."

"You can just call from different numbers, right?"

"Probably. I haven't tried it because I didn't have her yet."

"He probably has fifty burners with different numbers and once someone calls, he tosses it," Jack said. "Smart." Unfortunately. "How did you find out where she lives?"

"Her address was on the website as well as her place of business."

Jack sat back with a thump. "Then why isn't her place flooded with would be fortune hunters?"

"I don't think the page has been up long. Like just a few hours ago."

"And you specifically were on the dark web to see this... why?"

Pullman shrugged. "I do—*did*—a lot of IT management for a large firm. I use the dark web for situational awareness and threat analysis. With specific information, I can take counter measures to make sure my company isn't vulnerable to those threats."

Jack raised a brow. Everything the man said was true. They

were running a background check on him as they sat there and should have that information shortly. "And in doing all of that, you came across this ad saying bounty hunter for hire and you decided you'd be a good fit for that job?"

Pullman flushed. "I may not look like the type, but she didn't look like she'd be too hard to handle."

Jack swallowed a shout of laughter at how wrong the man was and refused to look at the mirror where Cheyenne sat watching. "How'd that work out for you?"

"I might have underestimated her a little," he muttered. "She got to that gun pretty fast. Scared me to death. Thought she was going to fill me with bullets."

"You would have deserved it, too, sneaking in her bedroom like that."

The guy shrugged. "Maybe so. And all that aside, honestly, I kind of wanted to warn her, too."

"Why?"

He hesitated, then ran a hand over his face. "Okay, I'll be straight with you. Yeah, something felt off. I even tried to pull up arrest records and see if she skipped bail. Now I know why I couldn't find anything on her." He shrugged. "But I needed the money, it all still looked legit, so I went for it. I don't know what she did or why someone is after her, but there are a lot of bad dudes out there who won't care if she's hurt in the process. I care. I wouldn't have hurt her. But some of those other guys? They will. If she's innocent and the bounty is really a hit, not the legit skipping-bail thing, then she's in big-time danger."

FOUR

She was in big-time danger. The thought overrode her indignation at the fact that Pullman thought she'd be an easy mark. The door opened and Cheyenne smiled at the woman who stepped inside. Early thirties, blue eyes, blond hair pulled back in a ponytail. Her badge read Amy Lee, Administrative Assistant. She was new, but she carried coffee so she was a potential BFF.

"Hi," the woman said, "thought you could use a cup." She passed it to Cheyenne who inhaled, then sipped. Needed more sugar, but the caffeine was perfect.

"Thanks."

"And you don't have any idea who is behind all of this?" Jack was asking. Cheyenne tuned back in.

Pullman shrugged. "No. I just came across the opportunity to make a lot of money and decided to take a chance."

"Okay, thanks." He stood. "You should call your lawyer. You're facing quite a few charges, possibly including attempted kidnapping since you basically stated that was your intention."

His face paled. "Oh, no. No. Please." He blew out a low breath and groaned. "I'm sorry. Really. I... It was stupid of me."

"And comes with consequences," Jack said, unsympathetic.

"I guess I should have checked everything out a little better."

"Yeah. You should have."

"I—uh—have the website address if you want it."

That was going to be Jack's next question. He grabbed a pen

and pad from the table in the corner and set them in front of the man. "I want it."

Once he had the information, Jack and the captain walked out of the room while West stayed to wrap things up with Pullman.

Cheyenne realized Amy was still there. She turned to the woman who'd been taking notes. "Sorry, I didn't mean to ignore you. I just wanted to hear what was going on."

"Of course." Amy smiled and tucked her pen and pad into her pocket. "It's fine. I'm getting ready to go to the academy so I like to sit in on the interrogations, try to learn something."

"Smart."

The woman smiled and headed for the door. "I'll see you later. Thanks for letting me stay."

"Sure thing. Thanks for the coffee."

Amy left and Cheyenne waited for the men to step inside. Jack raised a brow at her. "Well? I guess you heard all that."

"I did. I don't want to press charges. I'm sure he realized what he was getting himself into and he cooperated nicely as far as I could tell. I think he's just a chump who got in over his head. Instead, I'm going to my office and I'm going to find that ad and do some digging. I might be able to track the IP address or something."

"Sounds good. Let's go."

She grabbed her purse and followed after them. Within minutes, she found herself suppressing a sudden surge of fatigue, but at her desk, fingers flying over the familiar keyboard, she rallied, pulling up the website on the dark web that Pullman had provided.

Only to come up empty. "It's gone," she said.

Jack shifted. "What do you mean it's gone?"

"I mean, there's no trace it ever existed."

"Can you get it back?" the captain asked.

"I should be able to." But after thirty minutes of using every skill she possessed, she still couldn't locate it. Cheyenne dropped her hands from the keyboard with a frustrated sigh. "It's gone.

Like, it's completely gone. Whoever took it down didn't leave a trace."

She looked up at Jack and his kind eyes met hers. "It's okay," he said. "I tried too, but I couldn't find anything either."

"You don't understand. Whoever this is, he's—or she's—really good. Incredibly good with super high-end tech skills. There aren't many of us out there."

"Can you think of who this might be?"

She bit her lip and gave a short nod. "Maybe. A couple. The one that comes to mind first and foremost is a man I went up against once upon a time before I helped put him in prison. He was incredibly skilled. Genius-level hacker." She gave a tiny shrug. "I just happened to be a little better than him that day and managed to track down his location and send law enforcement to grab him."

"Who?"

"Travis Merrick."

"Check and see if you can find him," Jack said.

She went back to the keyboard and accessed the Plains City police and prison records. Then gasped. "He's out."

"When?"

"He was released last week."

"And you think it was him?"

"Well, I don't know for sure, but yeah, if he's out, he's the one I would point the finger at. When he was sentenced, I was there in the courtroom, and he vowed to get revenge. I wasn't worried. He was going to prison for a long time."

"So, how is he out?"

More searching turned up the reason. "His lawyer found a technicality in his arrest, and he was released." She banged a fist on the table and they all jumped. "Sorry, but I should have been notified immediately. Why didn't someone tell me?"

The captain shook his head. "I don't know, Cheyenne, but now we know, and we can act accordingly. I think it's best if you stay in a safe house for the time being."

"But—"

"No buts," Jack said. "This guy doesn't play."

"But it might not be him."

"Who are the others?"

She ran those names through and found each person where they were supposed to be. In prison.

She sat back and stared at the screen, processing. "Travis Merrick is the only one out."

"Could you be missing someone? Forgetting someone?"

"No. I made it a point to remember everyone who ever made a threat against me. I have no doubt the man who's behind everything is Merrick."

"Then the safe house is your only option right now."

Cheyenne swallowed. Then nodded. "All right. I'll go, but I want all my technology with me. I know how to keep him from tracking me wherever we land. Because I'm going to figure out where he is before he can find me." She turned back to the keyboard while the captain got on his phone to make the arrangements.

She could do this. Pulling on all her knowledge and skills, she went at it. Searching and coming up on dead ends, backing up and rerouting. It took her about twenty minutes, but she finally found it. An older and incomplete version of the website. It had basically nothing on it, but a weak SQL injection.

"You're kidding," Jack said.

She looked up. "Did I say that out loud?"

"You did," the captain said. "Someone want to tell me what a weak SQL injection is?"

Jack nodded to Cheyenne. "Go for it."

She frowned, trying to think of the best way to explain it. "Okay, imagine the website has a lock and your username and password are the key. We've all done that a bazillion times."

"Right, easy enough."

"Okay, SQL is the gatekeeper. It makes sure your key is the right one for the lock. But if the website isn't designed so that it's careful when checking keys, I or someone else can simply use a fake key and open the door."

The captain nodded. "Got it."

She tapped a few more keys. "And so I did. I'm looking around this web page I found and while I think it was linked to the one that disappeared, I'm not finding any kind of database or real information that might help. It looks like this was a draft before anything substantial was entered." She sighed. "Sorry."

"No need to be sorry," Jack said, his voice soft, "you're amazing."

The look in his eyes sent her heart tripping into a faster rhythm. "Jack—" His phone buzzed. "It's Daniel. He's ready to head to the safe house if we are."

Cheyenne frowned, but said, "Ready." Ready to talk to Daniel about his terrible timing, but that would have to wait, too. Right now, she needed to find the man who'd put a bounty—no, a *hit*—on her head.

Jack and Beau, with Daniel Slater and his Great Dane, Dakota, had successfully escorted Cheyenne to the safe house yesterday, which brought Jack some relief. It was in the middle of a wooded area that felt like one was all alone in a vast wilderness. In truth, Plains City was only about a fifteen-minute drive down the mountain, but the location was perfect with good visibility of the perimeter.

The captain had asked Jack to be her bodyguard and Daniel went along so they could take shifts. Some of the other team members would also be in and out, watching over her while she worked to find Merrick. Because in the time that Cheyenne had come up with him as a possibility to when they set foot in the safe house, no one could locate the man. It was like he'd dropped off the planet. When they'd gotten to the safe house last night, they all agreed it was best to get some sleep and pick up it again in the morning.

Now it was morning and the night had been, thankfully, quiet, but Jack had heard Cheyenne stirring around six thirty. He now stood in the doorway of the kitchen and watched her focus on setting up her workstation with Christmas music piping through the speaker on her phone.

Upon arrival last night, Beau and Dakota had sniffed every corner of the place, checking out the new smells. Jack smiled down at his partner. Beau and all the K-9s were amazing creatures, smart and eager to please those they loved. Beau lay in front of the couch on the shaggy rug he'd claimed as his while Dakota and Daniel scoped the outside perimeter. "You should have slept later this morning," Jack said. "You didn't get much sleep last night."

"I'll sleep when I have Merrick behind bars again. No one's safe with him on the outside. He's planning something. I mean, he obviously wants me delivered to him for some revenge plan he's got brewing, but I can guarantee you he has something else going on, too." She studied him for a brief second. "And besides, I don't think you got much, either."

"I got enough. Coffee helps."

"I had some, but could use another cup. Or five."

He chuckled. "I can get one of those for you." He left and brewed her a cup, added the required four teaspoons of sugar and a splash of milk from the fully stocked refrigerator. Daniel and Dakota came in. The dog went to her water bowl in the corner and lapped while Daniel locked the door behind him, then pulled off his gloves and hat and shrugged out of his coat. "It's quiet," he said to Jack. "No sign we were followed."

"Good."

"I brought the chess game."

Jack laughed. "Of course you did. Set it up. We can play in between watching windows and perimeter checks."

"Perfect."

He carried the coffee to Cheyenne and she took the cup, then a generous sip before setting it aside. She connected a cable to the large monitor. "Tell me about Merrick," he said. "I didn't work his case."

"He's an interesting guy." She brushed a few strands of dark hair from her eyes. "Total sociopath. Absolutely brilliant when it comes to all things techy. He could have done great things with his skills."

"Unfortunately, not everyone has that desire," Jack murmured.

"True. He grew up in a wealthy household. His father was a banker who made some very smart investments that paid off. His mother was involved in some charities in name only but spent most of her time hobnobbing with high society people." More cables connected brought more screens to life.

"You make it look so easy," Jack said. "Like you could hook all that together blindfolded."

She laughed. "I probably could." She side-eyed him. "You probably could too."

He doubted it. "Sorry. Go on."

"So, they lived life in the fast lane, had several homes around the world—including one here in Plains City, a private jet and pilot, and a chef that traveled with them. They kept their yacht off the coast of San Diego. Merrick has a brother, Jed, who is a pastor in a small town in Wisconsin. The two couldn't be more different. Anyway, two years ago, there was an attempted hacking of the town's banking system. Banks started reporting problems and it was brought to me to figure it out."

"I remember that. It was terrifying. And you figured it out? That was you? Why have you not told me this before?"

She shrugged. "I don't know. I haven't really thought about it since. But yes, I found Merrick was behind it. It took a lot of fancy maneuvering, but I discovered his hiding place, and the FBI working with the local PD went in and grabbed him—just in time to stop him from cleaning out all the local banks."

"I'd heard something about that." He had, but it was intriguing to hear it from the woman who'd been responsible for stopping the man.

"Jed went to see him in the prison and then came to see me after. I was skeptical of his intentions and sincerity at first, but the man has truly worked hard to separate himself from his family. He made sure I understood he was not like his brother or parents."

"You really believe that?"

She nodded. "I do. His sincerity wasn't an act as far as I could tell and he's done nothing but cooperate with law enforcement in all things related to his brother."

"I'm going to get in touch with him and ask if he's heard from Merrick. Maybe even send the authorities to his house to question him."

"I was going to suggest that. While you're doing that, I'm going to go digging and see what I can find. I have a sneaking suspicion that Merrick is already up to his old tricks. Not just to get revenge but possibly to make sure I'm out of the way so I can't stop him again."

Jack looked at her, admiration, respect and attraction all swirling within him for this woman. She was beautiful not just on the outside, but the inside as well. He'd had a big crush on her for a long time, and listening to her, worrying about her, desperate to find who wanted to hurt her, hurled his emotions onto a whole other level. He longed to reach out, pull her to him and tell her—

No. He moved that certain way just to see...

Yep, there it was. That pain that reminded him he could lose his leg. The pain he hadn't confessed to anyone, not even his closest friends. No one knew and he planned to keep it that way. Until he couldn't. If he lost his leg, he'd lose his career. The uncertainty clung like an albatross. Asking someone to deal with that because she was in a relationship with him wasn't an option. He grimaced and turned away from her. Wanting what he couldn't have. Well, that was par for the course, wasn't it? Not in his professional life anymore now that he was back on active duty, but when it came to his personal life...

Stop it.

What was he doing? He never wallowed in his past. So he hadn't grown up with loving parents and a family who supported him. Just a dictator father and mother desperate for the next prescription pill she could con someone into prescribing for her. He'd overcome that and made something of himself in spite of his rough beginnings. He had a good life and deserved to share that with someone. Didn't he?

And that frustrated him. Of course, as things progressed in a relationship, there was always the when-do-I-get-to-meet-your-parents thing that would eventually come up. And the answer, never, probably wouldn't go over too well. Ugh.

"...found something."

Cheyenne's voice brought him back to the present. He walked over to her and Beau looked up from his spot near the fireplace. When no one ordered him to work, he lowered his nose back to his paws and closed his eyes.

Daniel looked up from his spot on the couch. "Anything?"

"I think so," Cheyenne said. "I think I figured out what Merrick is doing."

"That didn't take you very long."

"It didn't. And it makes me a little suspicious, but nevertheless, if this is what he's planning, then we've got our work cut out for us."

"What's he planning?"

"To hit the banks again. It's the same plan he had before, just with an added element. He's not just going to steal from the banks in Plains City, but destroy them completely after he takes everything." She looked him in the eye, face pale. "And make it look like I did it."

FIVE

"How is that even possible?" Jack asked.

Cheyenne scanned the screen, then clicked on a link that brought up her picture and an IP address she recognized as her home. "This is how. He's manipulated everything to make it look like I'm tampering with the banking system from my home—" she clicked again "—and work IP address."

"He can do that?"

"Yes. It's not easy for the average person, but for him? It's nothing." She raked a hand over her hair and studied the information. "I've seen this kind of thing before. Not this exact thing, but I told you that before I joined the police force, when I was in school, I volunteered at a women's shelter and helped someone whose identity was stolen. My tech skills in this area have only gotten sharper since then."

"Good for you," Jack said.

Cheyenne sat back. "This isn't good, Jack."

"I gathered. Can you figure out where he is so we can nab him?"

"I don't know. He's good. Like very—"

An explosion from the kitchen rocked the house and smoke poured into the room. Beau barked and Cheyenne found her biceps gripped in Jack's powerful hands as he pulled her toward the exit.

"Get out!" Daniel's shout echoed. He and Dakota appeared

from the kitchen area, coughing. Dakota sneezed and shook her head. Daniel pointed. "Go out the kitchen door and into the garage. It's smoky, so hold your breath and run for it. Use the garage exit and head to the woods. We're right behind you."

Just as they reached the door, another object burst through the den window, spinning them around. Glass sprayed and the object landed on the carpet, smoke billowing to the ceiling and quickly filling the area.

"Go!" Jack's order spurred her to the kitchen. She held her breath as ordered and aimed herself for the door behind Jack and Beau. Daniel and Dakota brought up the rear. Jack threw the door open and, with a quick glance around, stepped out and went to the left. He led them out of the garage into fresh air and Cheyenne gulped it while she kept going. Another explosion sounded behind them.

And another.

They finally reached the edge of the woods and both dogs coughed and sneezed while the rest of them did the same.

Daniel pulled out a sat phone. "I'll call this in now that we have a chance to breathe, but keep an eye out for whoever just tried to fry us."

Cheyenne coughed into her sleeve and decided right then she was throwing the shirt away. "I don't think he was trying to kill us."

"What do you mean?" Jack asked.

She nodded to the house. "It was mostly smoke. I didn't see flames, did you guys?"

They exchanged a look. "No," Jack said, "I didn't."

Daniel shook his head. "Me, either. So no Molotov cocktail?"

"I don't think so," Cheyenne said. "Not the fiery kind, anyway. Follow me, but stay low and out of sight of the front of the house." She took off, anxious to see if she was right. The roar of an engine reached her and she picked up the pace. She rounded the corner of the house—that was still smoking, but definitely not burning—in time to see a van speed down the dirt road toward the main highway.

Jack and Beau arrived beside her. Then Daniel and Dakota. "He was waiting on us to come out," Daniel said.

Cheyenne nodded. "I think so. Just like the others, he wanted to grab me, not kill me. Smoking me out would do the trick. When no one came out the door, he must have gotten nervous and took off."

Jack blew out a low breath. "Yeah, you could be right."

Sirens sounded and within minutes they were surrounded by law enforcement. After they gave their statements and a description of the van, they returned to the house. Jack shook his head. "Obviously, we can't stay here. Cheyenne, is the tech stuff still usable?"

She examined it for the next several minutes, then looked up. "Yes. Surprisingly, nothing hit it. I mean it stinks, but it works."

"I'm not doubting your skills, but is there any way he tracked us with the technology we brought?"

She shook her head. "No way." Then hesitated. "I mean, I can't think how, but I suppose it doesn't mean he didn't manage to somehow bypass all my security." She paused. "Do I have time to look it all over?"

"Can you breathe in here?" Daniel asked.

"I'll manage." She sat at the desk and squinted through the remaining smoke, trying not to breathe too deeply. Someone handed her a mask and an air tank. She slipped it on and inhaled, grateful.

She stared at the screens, thinking, running through everything in her mind, then she went over all the equipment, searching through the software she'd used, looking for any kind of tracker that could have revealed her location.

She really couldn't find a weak link, but had Merrick? A wave of uncertainty shook her and she had to shake it off with the thought, *If he did, it won't happen again.* She continued to scan, clicking through every place she could think of. "I can't find a thing, but I'll go over it with a fine-tooth comb once we get to the next place."

He nodded. "All right then, let's grab all of our stuff while we have a police escort. We'll slip out and head to another safe house and see if we can find this guy."

"And how he knew how to find me," Cheyenne said.

Jack stroked Beau's ears. "Yes. Because if we know that, we can make sure it doesn't happen again."

He'd really like to know how they'd been compromised at the safe house. No one but their captain, Daniel and some of the team—people he worked with and trusted with his life—knew the location of the home. With this next one, it would be quite a few less. He'd taken a moment to try to track down Jed Merrick, but so far the man hadn't called him back. He'd also put in a call to the police department in Jed's small Wisconsin town and they hadn't called him back, either. While he waited, they'd move.

Captain Ross gave him the address and Cheyenne, Jack, Daniel and the dogs set off for it with Daniel and Dakota in a vehicle behind them to watch their backs. Cheyenne sat in the front seat winding the strap of her purse around her fingers and staring absently out the window, completely lost in thought. Beau's area was open in the back and he had his head between the seats resting on Cheyenne's shoulder. Jack watched her from the corner of his eye. "You okay?"

"Mm-hmm."

"It's all right if you're not. You've had a really trying couple of days."

"Mm-hmm."

"I know it's a lot to process. You could probably use some downtime."

"Mm-hmm."

"And I think we should fly to Hawaii and get married."

"Mm—what?" She snapped her head to look at him.

He grinned, trying to cover up his embarrassment that he'd

let those words fall from his lips. "I was just making sure you were listening."

"Uh, okay. Right. Well, I was thinking."

"I noticed."

She side-eyed him. "Hawaii?"

He shrugged, refusing to acknowledge the heat that had to be in his cheeks. "Yes. I've never been and—never mind. What were *you* thinking?"

"When I was in the hospital, you mentioned using me as bait to catch Merrick. We haven't gone that route. I think we should."

He grimaced. "Yeah, that probably wasn't the best idea I've ever had. Hiding you away and letting you find him with your skills is a much safer—i.e., *better*—plan."

She chewed her lip for a minute. "Pullman said that the bounty hunters get one call once they have me in their clutches."

"Yes."

"He hasn't made that call yet. We could use his burner to call Travis Merrick and arrange the drop-off and grab him once he shows."

Jack tapped the wheel, made a left and started to climb the winding mountain road. "I considered that."

"You did?"

"But again, that puts you in danger because I feel sure he's going to require that he sees you before anyone else sees him." He shrugged. "And it could be that he plans to kill anyone who brings you to him."

"Getting rid of any loose ends?" she asked, her voice low.

"Exactly. He doesn't know we know it's him. Yet."

"I still think it would work. Use Pullman's phone to call him and say you have me." She paused. "He'll probably want proof like a picture so we'll have to set that up, make it look real with me tied to a chair and a gag."

"I don't like it."

"I can't say I'm in love with it, but…"

"I think once we're settled in the new place…" he checked

the GPS "...that's ten minutes away, you can get set up with the equipment and try again."

She sighed. "Okay, fine. But if that doesn't work, then we have to try the plan, okay?"

"We'll cross that bridge when we come to it."

She wrinkled her nose, but dropped the subject. Her fingers twisted together, then she rubbed her palms on her jeans. Then clasped her hands once more. He reached over and covered her hands with his and she stilled. "It's going to be okay, Cheyenne. We're going to catch him and you're going to be fine."

She nodded. "I know." She let out a low breath.

"Tell me what you're thinking."

Looking out the window, she didn't answer him for a moment and he wondered if she'd share. Finally, she gave a little shrug. "I've been in law enforcement for a good length of time and I've chased down bad guys with full-on focus, not even worried about retaliation, but I have to admit, this situation is unnerving. He only knows who I am because I had to testify in court. He had a very good lawyer and the guy made me come in and show step by step how I tracked him down. I don't think his lawyer expected me to be so clear to the jury how I did it. That I was able to make them understand the complicated process. I think he figured I'd confuse them to the point of exasperation and they'd write me off. But they didn't. Merrick vowed he'd get revenge that day. I've kind of been looking over my shoulder ever since, but I don't think I really thought he'd actually have the opportunity to do it."

"I know, but we're going to stop him again before he can do anything. There's no other option."

"Right. Sure."

She sounded like she didn't believe it, but like he'd said, there wasn't any other choice. Because he wasn't losing Cheyenne—or the possibility of a future with her. And then his leg twinged and the doubts crept back in. No, not today. No doubts. Not on his end, anyway. But Cheyenne had them. Before his injury, they'd danced around each other, the attraction there, the desire to be more than friends obvious to both of them. Cheyenne had been the one to keep things between them surface level in spite of the fact he could tell she wanted more, too. What it boiled down to was they both had to move past their fears and be willing to take the risk that came with being vulnerable. He was willing. He just had to figure out how to make sure she was all in with that plan, too.

SIX

I think we should fly to Hawaii and get married.

Cheyenne frowned, but kept her snort to herself. *Who says that?*

A guy who wasn't interested, but thought he was being cute with his teasing? Or who had no idea a girl had a massive crush on him so didn't even think about how his words might make her feel? Or he knew and just didn't know how to deal with it?

It *could* be that last one, but she just wasn't sure. He was definitely in all-out protection mode that made it *seem* like he cared for her more than a friend, but she sure didn't want to *assume*. Gah, what a disaster that could be.

She wished he'd just come right out and tell her how she fit in his life—friend or more than, or just coworker. If it was the last one, then fine. She just wanted to know so she could process the hurt, grieve for what wouldn't be and move on.

She picked nonexistent lint from her jeans. Then stopped and looked at him out of the corner of her eye. No, he was interested, but something was holding him back. Just like something had been holding her back before his injury. And still was, if she was being honest. Falling in love with Jack was a big risk for her. If something went wrong and they wound up going their separate ways, would she lose the rest of the friend group who'd become family to her? She couldn't fathom it.

Then again, it was looking more and more like her heart thought Jack might be worth the risk.

She could just ask him how he felt about her, right? But that would be awfully awkward, wouldn't it? *You're used to awkward, Cheyenne, why not lean into it?* "Jack?"

"Yes?"

"Um…how do you…" She paused. Nope. No. She couldn't. "What made you decide to go into law enforcement? Be a K-9 handler?" She refused to groan out loud. She was such a chicken.

He hesitated. Swallowed. Glanced at her. And flexed his fingers around the wheel. "That's a loaded question."

"Really? I wouldn't think it would be that difficult."

He sighed. "On the surface, it's not."

"Oh. Okay." She glanced at him. He seemed deep in thought about something. Like he was trying to make a decision that was painful. Like talking about what was beneath the surface?

"So, my dad was a fire chief for Plains City. Worked a lot of hours, was rarely home. Saved lives on a regular basis. He was a hero in everyone's eyes."

"From your tone, I'm guessing not so much in yours?"

He shot her a quick glance as though surprised she'd read him so well. "Right. Not so much in mine. My mom was—is—a junkie. And my dad…it was his way or the highway. He didn't delegate, he dictated. I… I hate to admit it, but I hated him growing up. I've worked through that. Now I just feel sorry for him. For both of them."

He snapped his lips shut like he regretted allowing the words to escape so she tried not to react too much. "I'm sorry. That sounds like a hard way to grow up."

"It was and it wasn't. On the surface, we looked like any other normal American family, so everyone treated us like one. That was nice. But beneath it all, we were paddling hard to keep up the facade."

"Will you see them for Christmas?"

He nodded. "I'll go by, take presents, make small talk, then my dad will say something about me getting a real job and that will be my cue to leave before it gets ugly."

"I'm so sorry."

Silence fell between them for a few moments, then he said, "But in answer to your question, one afternoon, I was at the county fair and there was a K-9 handler with his dog there. I was fourteen years old and followed them around the place for probably thirty minutes. It was a drug dog and I watched them make a bust. When everything settled down, the handler spotted me still watching and finally asked me if he could answer any questions I might have. I asked every question I could think of and for an hour he told me all about what it was like being a handler, what classes to take in school and so on. His name is Peter Billings. He's retired and runs a training facility in Florida, but we still talk every so often."

"Wow. He sounds amazing."

"He is. Anyway, I managed to survive my teenage years, got a scholarship to college and majored in criminal justice. The rest, as they say, is history." He paused. "Mom still has her drug problem and Dad still wants to run my life. I've tried to help Mom, but she doesn't want it. I've come to accept that. For now. I still check in on her and my dad, but we don't see other much."

"I'm really sorry about that."

"I am, too, actually. Maybe things will get better eventually. I pray for it."

She studied him. "Why haven't you told me that before and why was that so hard for you to share with me now?"

He snapped a look at her, then back to the road. "Really?"

"Yeah."

"Maybe for the same reasons you didn't share with me about how hard your growing up years were with your parents?"

"Huh." She blinked. "What did we even talk about in the months before you were shot?"

"I know your favorite food is fettuccine Alfredo with grilled chicken and that you hate cherries and anything flavored with it. You love dogs, are allergic to cats and are an only child. Just to name a few things."

All true. "We talked about those things?"

"Some. Some I just observed."

He paid attention. Her cheeks warmed. Then again, he was a cop, so...

But maybe his observations meant more?

She circled back to her original idea of simply asking him what she meant to him.

Just say it.

It could make things awkward.

Or it could answer a lot of questions.

She shut off the internal argument and cleared her throat. "I...ah...want to ask you something, but I'm not sure how." He raised a brow at her and she shook her head. "Okay, here goes. Before you were shot—and this may totally be from my perspective and it could be very wrong—but I thought we were... getting closer. And I know I probably sent mixed signals because of my own insecurities, but I just want you to know I was enjoying hanging out with you, talking—" *dating?* "—and then after you were shot..." She shrugged. "I don't know. Something changed between us. I mean, I understand you getting shot and your long recovery was a major thing so I don't want you to think I'm belittling that or not giving it the attention—" She stopped. "Okay, I'm going to shut up now before I embarrass myself further. I just wanted to know if something changed." She paused. "No, I want to know *what* changed." She snapped her lips together and stared out the window, trying not to cringe, praying she didn't sound pathetic.

He reached over with his right hand and snagged her left. "Hey, you're right. Something changed, but it wasn't anything you said or did." She whipped her head around to look at him. "We're here, but I promise we'll continue this conversation at the first possible moment, all right?" She looked down. "Cheyenne, please? I appreciate you finally opening up to me and being vulnerable. I know that was hard." He swallowed and then glanced in his rearview mirror. "We're practically at the safe house and Daniel is right behind us, so I'll do the same as soon as we have a chance and some privacy. I promise."

With another ragged breath, she nodded and looked him in the eye. "Yeah. Okay." Why had she waited so long to say something and then decided to say it when they were finally at their destination? There was probably some deep-seated psychological reason behind that, but she had no time to decipher it. She sighed. "Let's go."

It didn't take long to get inside and get everything set up once again. This time, instead of going straight to work, Cheyenne needed some time alone to process—especially after that conversation in the car that they were not acknowledging at the moment—and to just...*be*. If she didn't, she wouldn't be able to think. And that was one thing she needed to do above all else. "It's been a long day. I'm afraid if I start working right now, I'll miss something. So I'm going to crash for the night, then I'll get to work early in the morning. Is that okay?"

"Of course. You can't be expected to work around the clock and still function. Get some sleep. Daniel and I'll take turns sleeping and keeping an eye out. The dogs will alert us, too, if anyone they don't know approaches."

She nodded and wondered when they'd continue the conversation. Hopefully when she was much more coherent than she felt at the moment. The adrenaline spike and crash had loosened her tongue earlier with Jack. If she didn't get some sleep, there was no telling what she'd say—and regret it later. "Night, guys."

"Night, Cheyenne."

Jack's soft voice followed her down the hallway. She swallowed at the surge of longing that swept through her. She wanted this mess to be over. She wanted to finish the conversation and hear what Jack had to say. She wanted to wrap her arms around him and kiss him senseless. But allowing that to happen would change everything. Hopefully for the good. Possibly for the bad.

And that small *possibly* shot enough darts of fear through the *hopefully* that she wished she could rewind time and start over with Jack. Do things different. Conquer her fear and be brave enough to tell the man she was crazy about him.

But first, they needed to catch the man responsible for all of the chaos sideswiping them.

Because if they didn't, she might not live to put aside her fear and learn to take a few risks in life.

The fact that the night and next morning passed peacefully was almost unnerving for Jack. He kept waiting for something to come flying through the window. Like a bullet. Or another smoke bomb. Thankfully, it was now lunchtime and Cheyenne had been hard at work for the past several hours. Their car conversation was still unfinished and weighing heavy on his mind. And his heart. But now wasn't the time to worry about it. Cheyenne had a job to do and he'd leave her alone to do it.

Dakota and Beau took turns begging for belly rubs and treats while he and Daniel had the chessboard out. It was Daniel's turn. The man moved his queen into position and sat back with a small smile. "Checkmate."

Jack face-palmed and shook his head. "That's twice you've beaten me without even halfway trying."

Daniel's gaze slid to Cheyenne. "You're a little distracted."

"I'm a lot distracted," Jack muttered and rose to walk to the window. Beau followed him. Why had he told her that stuff about his family? It was like he lost his filters when it came to her. But she'd asked and he wasn't going to lie. Could have been a little more vague, but she would have seen right through that. And she was right. They had been getting closer. Hanging out, getting to know one another outside of work. They hadn't called it dating, but he'd been about to say something about it when he'd been shot. And things had definitely changed. He'd become withdrawn and pushed her away, appalled for her to see him so weak.

Yeah, it was stupid. His dumb pride had hurt her. And him,

too, if he was going to keep up with this whole being-honest-with-himself thing.

A gasp came from Cheyenne and he turned. She was staring at the screen like she'd never seen one before. He walked over to her. "What is it?"

"I found it. I found the malware and how he's going to use it to destroy the city's banking system."

"That's great. Can you disable it?"

She frowned, her top teeth clamped onto her bottom lip. He wanted to reach out and free it before she hurt herself. That thought sent his fingers curling into a fist. Not his place, not his right. He just wanted it to be.

Wow. Focus, man.

She shook her head. "I don't know. It's good. It's very good."

"But not better than you."

She shot him a quick smile before her gaze returned to the screen. "I'm not so sure about that."

"I am." And he was. "You got this."

"But no pressure, right?"

"None at all." He paused. "Okay, maybe a little."

For the next few hours, she worked. Then stopped. Jack looked up from the third chess game he and Daniel had been in the middle of. "What?"

"I think I found him."

Jack pulled his phone out. "Where?"

"It's a warehouse downtown." She clicked a few more keys. "It's empty, but for sale along with several other properties in the area."

"Give me the address and we'll dispatch a team."

"Sent it."

Over the next hour, they planned their next move. Jack hung up. "All right. We have the team. SWAT is on the way. And Beau and I are going, too."

She nodded. "I figured they'd want you. Merrick deals in technology. It's likely Beau will come in handy."

"I'm going to take one more walk around the perimeter before you leave," Daniel said. "I'll be back."

He left them alone and Jack decided to take advantage of the opportunity. He walked over to her and took her hands. "Cheyenne, we didn't get to finish our conversation and it's not one I wanted to have in front of Daniel, but I… I have a lot of baggage. Stuff I'm not sure it's fair to ask another person to deal with, but—" He sighed. *Come on, man, spit it out.* "But, I want to at least talk about it. And then see where we stand."

Where they stood? Did that really just come out of his mouth?

But she wasn't laughing. She simply nodded. "Let's talk as soon as we can. As soon as all of this is settled. For now, just be safe."

"Okay. Good. Yeah, we'll be safe." He let his gaze drift to her lips. It would be so easy to lean over and—

No. No way. Not yet. There was too much that needed saying first. But if it all worked out like he wanted it to…

He shut off that thought, too. And sighed. At this point, he wasn't going to be able to think at all. He stepped back. "I'll be in touch. Stay safe."

She watched him go and he just prayed he could return and tell her all was well. But there was a small niggling at the base of his skull that said he'd better not count his chickens before they hatched.

SEVEN

It was quiet at the safe house. Too quiet. Daniel and Dakota continued to keep watch while Cheyenne pushed aside the desire to come up with a way to get Jack alone and finish their conversation about what had changed. Unfortunately, her personal life was on hold indefinitely thanks to Merrick.

So she worked and tried to forget that she thought Jack had almost kissed her. It was hard, but she did it because she had to.

She managed to get into the warehouse security system even though it had been turned off—which she thought was odd. Turning it back on had been a little tricky, but thankfully the power at the warehouse was still connected, so she'd succeeded without too much hassle.

Getting into the cameras had been no problem, but only one was working. Again, weird. She gave access instructions to the tech person in the van on the curb since she'd figured it out before him. "You're amazing, Cheyenne," the guy said. "It's a good thing you want to use your skills for good. Otherwise, we'd all be in trouble."

She laughed and ignored the heat climbing up her neck and into her cheeks, grateful he couldn't see her face. "Thanks." What else could she say? "But before I take credit, just know that I'm finding this all a bit too easy. The alarm system was off. I find that troubling, so be careful, okay? I can only think of one reason the system would be down and that's because it's some kind of trap."

"10-4."

While she waited for the team to get to the warehouse, she kept an eye on the camera, desperate to see any movement or proof that Merrick was there.

So far nothing.

She picked up the satellite phone and debated calling Jack for an update, then set it aside. When he had something to tell her, he would.

"I'm going to check the perimeter again," Daniel said from the foyer. "Dakota and I'll be right back."

"Thank you." Cheyenne looked at him. "I appreciate you doing this."

"Of course. I wouldn't be anywhere else."

"I'm not quite sure I believe that." She smiled. "I haven't talked to Aurora lately. How are she and Joy doing?" Aurora was Daniel's fiancée and they were adopting Daniel's three-year-old niece, Joy, together. Joy's father wasn't in the picture and the little girl's mother had passed away after an illness.

"They're great."

"Planning the wedding?"

"Yes. And it can't come soon enough if you ask me."

"I'm sure." She turned back to the screen. "Thank you again. Dakota should get extra treats for this duty."

"I'm sure she'd agree." He clicked to the dog to follow him. "We'll be back."

He left and Cheyenne tapped the mouse to maneuver around the warehouse again, using the one camera to see if anything had changed.

Nothing had.

She blew out a low breath and rubbed her nose. *God, please let this end soon. Let them catch Merrick so I—we—can get on with our lives. And help me conquer my fear.*

She continued the prayer until a sound from the kitchen

caught her attention and she turned. "Daniel?" Why would he come in that way when he'd just left out the front a couple of minutes ago? He usually took longer to do the check.

He didn't answer and she tensed. A man—not Merrick—stepped into the den and pointed a gun at her. "You have two minutes to cooperate with me. Otherwise, I shoot the dude walking the dog over by the fence line."

Cheyenne stood, hands up. Her weapon was on the desk and within reach, but did she dare even try?

As though he read her mind, he gestured with the gun. "Don't think about it. The clock is ticking. I've been watching for the past few hours and soon, he's going to be coming in that front door. I'll pick him off easy-peasy and you'll be going with me, anyway."

"Who are you?" She noted he was about six foot five inches, big bushy red beard, green eyes and long hair to match the beard. He didn't seem to care that she could identify him and that scared her.

A lot.

"Someone who needs the bounty on your head," he said.

"A killer put it there."

"I don't care who put it there as long as they pay. Now, put your hands up and keep your mouth shut. As long as you don't alert him, he lives. It's your choice."

A deep tremor started within her. A fear like she'd never known sent panic clawing its way from her gut to her throat. What did she do? "All right. I'll go with you."

She walked over to him, then past him. The gun dug into her left kidney and she gritted her teeth. "Out the door," he said, "to the left and around the side of the house. Follow the path into the woods. I have a car waiting. Go. If he sees you, he'll try to stop you. And that makes him dead."

Daniel was somewhere close by. If she called out to him, would this man really shoot him? She sized him up in seconds. Kidnapping was one thing. Murder was in a whole other category, but yes, she thought he might, so she couldn't take the chance. Aurora and Joy needed Daniel. But he'd soon discover her missing and immediately start the search. He'd alert Jack and they'd find her.

But how?

She continued to follow her abductor's instructions, keeping her hands where he could see them. "Hurry up," he said.

Cheyenne picked up the pace a fraction while forcing herself to stay calm and running self-defense scenarios in her head. Her abductor was big. Very big. And strong. She could take him down, but she'd have to rely on brains, outsmart him. The main goal was to separate him from the gun. Without the weapon, Daniel would be okay.

"Hey! Stop right there!"

Daniel's call twirled her around and face-to-face with the man trying to take her. The gun moved from her side to her nose. "Make it a three-sixty or I shoot him," he said through gritted teeth. Daniel was too far away to be any help at the moment, but if she could delay...

Her kidnapper snagged her arm and yanked her toward the sedan parked ten yards ahead. "I'm not playing."

He wasn't. Heart pounding, she went. She couldn't let him shoot Daniel, but she wasn't about to get in a car with this guy, either. She walked as slow as possible, hoping Daniel had a clear view of what was happening. Her lagging earned her a shove forward. She stumbled, but kept upright and continued on the path the man indicated.

"Cheyenne! Stop!"

Her abductor yanked her to a stop and whirled, keeping her between him and Daniel. "Come any closer and she's dead!" He jerked her arm. "Warn him I'm serious. Tell him to throw the gun away right now."

"Daniel, stop! Don't do it! I'll be okay. He says to toss your gun now."

Daniel slowed, hands clamped around the grip of his weapon.

The guy behind her pulled her arm up hard enough to make her yelp.

"Now!" His shout echoed in her ear.

Daniel tossed the gun and held up his hands.

"Let's go," the man growled at her and stepped back. She whirled with a roundhouse kick and caught the guy in the knee while she ducked away from the barrel of the gun. Dakota's bark said she was on the way to help.

Curses rang from her abductor and before she could go on the attack with another kick, a hard smash to the left side of her head just above her temple stunned her long enough for him to snap her wrists into a pair of handcuffs. Her ear rang and nausea swirled.

Daniel's frantic calls faded and the man behind her maneuvered her into the back seat of his car.

The engine roared and Cheyenne struggled into a sitting position only to realize she was in the back of a car—outfitted like a police vehicle—with a divider system keeping her from accessing her captor. She banged on the plexiglass. "Where are you taking me?"

"To get my two hundred fifty grand. Now shut up and enjoy the ride."

Jack's phone vibrated just as he and Beau entered the warehouse with the rest of the team. He ignored the call, praying it wasn't an emergency. They'd been warned it could be a trap and he needed all his focus on this moment. Everything else had to wait.

The scent of dust and printer ink registered. Jack held his weapon ready and directed Beau to search while everyone fanned out, rifles held to their chins, goggles over their eyes, their gear a protection against most assaults. The lights cast long shadows on the concrete floor and Jack watched for anything that might indicate a booby trap. Beau aimed himself to the office area, tucked away in the far corner, his nose quivering with every new smell.

The three-wall glass perimeter afforded Jack the luxury of seeing inside before making entry. The fourth wall, directly opposite him, was Sheetrock. He led Beau to the open glass door and scanned the interior. It was a small space, furnished with a desk pushed against the solid wall. An overturned desk chair lay in front of the file cabinet that held open drawers. Papers littered the floor as if someone had been searching for something, then left in a hurry. There was nothing to indicate if they'd found what they were looking for. Or maybe they'd been cleaning out evidence they *didn't* want found?

Through his comms, he heard, "Clear," several times. Beau sniffed the doorframe, then moved inside. Jack followed, his eyes scanning the room once more. Beau's attention focused on the desk and he trotted over, ears perked forward. He nosed the bottom drawer and sat, looking up at Jack expectantly, tongue hanging out the side of his mouth. His alert. "Pleased with yourself, huh? Good boy."

Jack eased the drawer open and looked inside. A single laptop. "Beau found something in the office."

"On the way."

He wasn't sure who was on the way, but he'd take any backup he could get. He took a closer look and was almost ready to pull the laptop from its resting place when he noticed a wire running from the laptop to the back of the drawer. And a flashing red light. When he'd opened the drawer, he'd triggered some kind of detonator. Terror spiked. "Guys, get out. I think we have a bomb here and it's rigged to blow. I don't know how long we have so get out now!"

He turned and Beau, sensing the sudden tension, barked and followed Jack as he ran from the office and across the warehouse floor, aiming them toward the exit. The others were streaming out of the building, too. Jack and Beau made it across the street before the explosion went off.

The blast was hard enough to send him to the ground. He wrapped his arms around Beau and rolled them behind the closest vehicle while debris rained down. A brick hit his good leg and bounced off. Pain radiated, but he stayed still, covering Beau. The dog waited, not struggling against the confinement. Seconds ticked away.

"Everyone report in!"

The command came through his comms and ringing ears and he responded with, "Donodio." He listened for the other names and closed his eyes in a brief moment of gratitude and prayer when it became clear no one had been injured or killed.

Then he looked around the side of the car and waited for another blast.

Time passed by with no more explosions.

Shouts and sirens mingled together. The fire trucks had been called as soon as he'd said the word *bomb* and thankfully hadn't wasted any time getting there. He released Beau and checked him over, running his hands over the dog's flanks, feet, tail. Every inch. "You're good, right, boy?"

Beau licked his face and sat. Jack leaned his forehead against the animal's and sent up silent prayers of gratitude. Not just for Beau's safety, but for everyone else as well.

His phone buzzed and he realized it had been buzzing for the past several minutes. He pulled it out of his pocket and glanced at the screen. Several texts from Daniel.

Call me.

Emergency.

Cheyenne kidnapped. Don't know where she's been taken.

EIGHT

Cheyenne struggled against the man who had her over his shoulder, face down, cuffed hands useless. His shoulder pressed into her diaphragm making it difficult to breathe and her head pounded from his punch. Five minutes after they'd taken off in the car from the safe house, he'd pulled over and blindfolded her.

Now he carried her down a flight of stairs and dumped her on the floor. She landed on her left hip with a hard thud, but managed to suppress a grunt. She shoved off her blindfold and scooted back, wanting the wall behind her—and distance from him.

"What now?" she asked, hating the slight tremor in her voice. Her head might explode and save him the trouble of killing her.

"He's supposed to meet me here," he said.

"Who?"

"The guy with the money. He's on his way." He turned to go.

"How did you find me?"

"I had a little help."

Well, that was mysterious. "From who?"

"Doesn't matter." He backed toward the stairs.

"Wait!"

He paused.

"The fact that he's going to kill me doesn't bother you?" she asked.

He frowned. "It bothers me, but without that money, I'm the

one who's dead, so I'm willing to figure out how to live with that."

"You don't know who he is," she said. "I do. I crossed him once and this is his revenge. And he hates loose ends so he's going to kill you, too, because you're...you know, a loose end."

He stilled and hope blossomed. He seemed to be thinking hard about her words. Then shook his head. "I borrowed money from some really bad people. Dealing with this guy is a risk I'm willing to take."

Fear clawed at her. "I'm telling you, you don't know what you're getting into. He's a killer. Doesn't think twice about it. You're so in over your head, you can see that helping me is your only hope and I'm trying desperately to convince you of that." As long as he was listening, she'd try to reach him.

The conflicted look, the hesitation, watching him rake a hand over his shaggy hair in indecision, sparked more hope, but he finally shook his head. "Sorry. I really am." And then he was racing back up the stairs. The click of the deadbolt echoed back at her and her fragile hope died a violent death. Just like she was going to do if she didn't get it together.

Her hands were still cuffed in front of her and panic threatened to overwhelm her along with the nausea from her pounding head. She closed her eyes for a moment and tried to slow her racing heartbeat.

Think, Cheyenne, think.

She was so *stupid*. She should have fought back harder, found a way to disarm him and distract him. Anything to help Daniel help her. Anything. But what if the guy had shot him? Then where would she be? First, she hadn't wanted Daniel harmed and second, at least he knew she was in trouble and would rally everyone to help find her. If he'd taken a bullet for her—which she knew he would have—then it would have been a much longer time between her snatching and the time she was discovered missing.

She just had to stay alive long enough to give the team the chance to find her.

"I'm sorry, Jack," she whispered. "I'm sorry I didn't tell you how I feel." She wanted to live if only to do that. Whether he responded in kind or not, at least he'd know. They could finish their conversation and she'd know. All of her worry about losing her people should she and Jack become an item and then break up was still a very real thing, but some things—some *people*—were worth the risk. She just hated it took her being in this situation to come to that realization, but hindsight was twenty-twenty and all that. No more time for regrets, wishes or reflection. It was time to act.

She used the wall to help her stand and, ignoring her aching head and queasy stomach, aimed herself toward the bathroom. She didn't know how much time she had, but she had to get the cuffs off.

She focused on the sink, her gaze locked onto the metal lever that controlled the drain plug. It was old and gross, covered with who knew what, but now wasn't the time to be squeamish. If she could get it out—or at least a piece of it—it might just be thin and sturdy enough to pick the lock.

Cheyenne knelt and looked at the exposed pipe underneath. It, too, was corroded and the pivot rod was halfway off. Maybe that would be the better choice.

With shaking fingers, she gripped the thing and tugged at it, moving it back and forth, twisting it, then pulling. Finally, a piece popped free. A small flat piece of metal about the thickness of a handcuff key. But it wouldn't work like that. "Please bend." Saying the words out loud fortified her. She moved to the stove and pressed her little piece of metal against the sturdy burner, desperate to shape what was left of the pivot rod into what she needed. Finally, she had it curved slightly. "Okay, God," she whispered, "here we go. Please let this work. Please, please, please."

She sat on the floor, her back against the wall and slid the piece of metal into the lock. She'd never picked locks before and had no idea what she was doing, but she'd read about this and knew she had to engage the release latch inside. She closed her eyes for a moment and sucked in a steadying breath, slowed her ragged breathing and went to work while keeping her ears tuned to any indication Merrick was there.

It would be so much easier if she could stop the trembling in her hands, but she didn't have time to figure out how to do that. She was freezing so that wasn't helping.

Focus.

After what felt like an eternity and a half, the lock gave way. She allowed herself a brief flash of elation before she wiggled her wrist and the cuff fell open. "Oh, thank you, Jesus. Thank you." She didn't bother with the other cuff. There was no way she had the time to spend on it like she had the first one.

Escape was her priority now.

Cheyenne flexed her wrists, rubbing the sore spots where the cuffs had dug into her skin, then tucked the metal piece into her front pocket.

Now to get out.

When Jack had read Daniel's text, he'd gone into shock, then anger, then guilt. He never should have left her. How had she been found? Daniel stood next to him, his face white, jaw tight. No doubt the man was feeling his own range of emotions since she'd disappeared on his watch. But it wasn't Daniel's fault. There was no blame to place on anyone except the person who'd orchestrated this.

Reeling, they'd called everyone who could help find Cheyenne to come to the safe house, then collected everything that belonged to her. That small pile was in the middle of the den. He and Beau, Daniel and Dakota, West Cole, and Jenna Morrow with Augie had descended on the safe house. Jack pointed to the computer station Cheyenne had set up and her meager belongings. "There's no way anyone tracked her through the computer. She's too good to leave a trail. So it has to be some kind of physical tracker. Beau, heel." He snapped his fingers at Beau and the dog hurried to his side. Jack pointed again to the items. "Search."

The dog sent his nose diving into the items. When he came to Cheyenne's purse, he whined, then sat. Jack looked at Jenna. "Okay, it could be anything, an SD card with pictures, whatever, but I'm going to need to know what Beau's alerting to. I'm not sure I feel too great about going through her personal things, do you mind? Look for some kind of tracker. Anything."

"Got it. Although, honestly, if it helps save her life, I don't think she's going to complain."

Jack raised a brow. "Agreed. But I'll let you do it anyway." Jenna pulled on a pair of gloves and took the purse. While she did that, Jack went through everything in the small suitcase she'd brought just because it seemed like the smart thing to do. She had clothes, a bag of makeup that he'd never seen her use, a book on chess—okay, that made his heart squeeze tight— toiletries, her Bible, a picture of her and people who had to be her parents. Simple and sparse. That was Cheyenne.

"Um," Jenna said, "I might have found it." She held something between her thumb and pointer finger. "There's nothing else in here that Beau would alert to. Her phone's missing, no cards, no flash drive, nothing."

"What is it?" Daniel asked, squinting.

She shrugged. "A tracker. I mean, I'm not up-to-date on every tracker ever made, but this looks like one to me."

"Who could have put that in there and when?" Jack asked. "Think."

"Walk us through everything," Jenna said, "starting with what you—and Cheyenne—were doing and where you were before the attacks started."

Jack frowned. "It started with someone trying to run Cheyenne off the road and she went to help him and found that flyer with the bounty on her head. She went to the hospital and was released, then Jenna and I watched her house that night and that's when we caught Pullman trying to break in." He hesitated. "But she didn't have any contact with Pullman. Like none. She stayed in the observation room."

"So who did she see between then and going to the safe house?"

Jack thought. "We were at the station and she watched the interrogation of Pullman. When we left the station, we went straight to the safe house."

"Any security footage of the wreck?" Daniel asked.

"A couple of ring doorbells on the road where the wreck happened, but nothing clear," Jenna said. "Just her car going by. And the dead guy's. Nothing with the actual wreck itself. We've already studied all of that."

Daniel sighed. "What about at the hospital?"

"We can get that and see who went in and out of her room," West said, "but it's going to take some time to go through that footage. I'll get it now." He got on his phone to put the call in.

Jack raked a hand through his hair. They didn't have time. "And then we were at the station," he said.

"The station." Daniel met his eyes. "I don't want to think it, but—"

"But yeah," Jack said, knowing where his friend was going. "We still have to check the security footage from there."

"Let's divide up," Jenna said. "We have enough laptops and can cover more footage faster that way."

"Perfect." They each logged into a device, pulled up the file with all of the footage that was thankfully labeled.

"I got the hospital footage," Jack said.

Daniel nodded. "I've got the first half of the station. Jenna, you start at about the halfway point."

"On it," she said.

West looked at Jack. "I'll do the same with the hospital footage and start at the halfway point."

"Perfect. At least we can run it fast until she comes on screen," he said. Hopefully that would allow the viewing to go even faster.

All Jack could do was pray and search. They had to find her alive and well. Because while he was still a little scared of what the future held as far as his leg, he was more scared of facing a future without Cheyenne. He got busy with the footage, desperately searching for something. He and Cheyenne had a conversation to finish so he needed anything that would tell him more about Merrick or where Cheyenne was. Her life depended on it.

NINE

Cheyenne had lost track of how much time had passed. She just knew that she hadn't found a way out yet and she was getting desperate. With the handcuffs banging on everything and getting in the way, she finally stopped and worked it off. They were now in her pocket ready to be used on Merrick should she have to find a way to incapacitate him.

She stood, hands on her hips, looking around. She'd searched everywhere and had one last idea for escape when footsteps overhead froze her for a quick minute. If that was Merrick, she was dead.

Her heart thudded and she moved to the far closet, opened it and stepped inside.

Only to feel something run across her foot. She clamped a hand over her mouth to hold in the scream. She didn't want to move, almost couldn't breathe. Which worked out okay since she really needed to listen. She hadn't closed the closet door completely and a sliver of light filtered in. Something glinted in the corner, catching her eye, and she reached out to close her fingers around the metal golf club.

Sheer relief almost brought laughter in spite of the rodents. Almost. Not yet. It wasn't an ideal weapon but it would work as good as anything else she'd be likely to find.

When there were no more sounds from above over several minutes, she crept up the steps to the locked door and listened.

A door slammed and all was quiet. For a moment, she stayed put, but truly it was now or never. She backed down a few steps and put the flat edge of the putter under the bottom hinge pin and pushed. It slid from the hole and fell to the step with a clatter. She held her breath. She hadn't expected it to come out so easy. With her nerves humming, she waited, listening, praying no one came to investigate the noise.

Thankfully, the silence was broken only by her ragged breathing and pounding heart. She was going to have permanent heart damage at this rate. Assuming she lived through this situation. She walked up one step and did this same for the middle pin. This time she was prepared and stopped when it was about three quarters of the way out. A sharp tug and it landed in her palm.

For a moment, she wondered how heavy the door was should it come tumbling down, but the other side was dead bolted so she could only pray it held. Then she stopped and considered she should probably leave the top pin in. Maybe?

Using the flat edge of the putter, she put pressure on the crack in line with the hinges, but it was too tight to maneuver. She tried the larger crack at the bottom and tugged toward her. The door separated from the bottom hinge with a scrape and once more she paused, senses on high alert. When nothing happened and no footsteps sounded, she moved back to the crack and continued the careful pressure upward until she had a wide enough space to reach under and grab it with both hands. With one last firm tug, the door came free of the middle hinge.

And gave her an opening wide enough to slip through.

If someone was watching the door, she was doomed. After several seconds of no footsteps or other noises to indicate she'd been caught, she peered out, confirming her suspicions that she was in a house. There was a washer and dryer to her right. Straight through the laundry room was the kitchen that led to a foyer. That was all she could see from her vantage point. She scooted through the opening and slid her hands under the bottom of the door to pull it back in place, hoping it would hide her escape well enough to buy her some time.

She crept to the open door that led into the kitchen, listening over the blood rushing through her veins and peered around the edge. It was a simple kitchen painted a pale yellow. It was also, thankfully, empty. The dining room was to her right. She walked into it and saw it opened into the den area that had a beautifully decorated Christmas tree in the corner next to the fireplace. Where was she? Whose house was this? No way could it be Merrick's, could it? While she moved through the home, she kept her eyes peeled for a landline or a discarded cell phone. A computer. Anything.

But nothing.

She had no idea where she was, but by her calculation, she was about thirty to forty minutes from the safe house. There should be computers and all kinds of electronics in this place if it was Merrick's, but all she could see was furniture and Christmas. Did she dare try to take a peek into the bedrooms?

A door slammed and she gasped, walked to the French doors off the small dining area and twisted the knob. She pushed.

It didn't open.

Footsteps entered the kitchen behind her.

She shoved harder and it gave, allowing her to dart out onto the deck and shut the door.

Only it didn't latch, and she had no time to try again.

Cold wind whipped around her and she shivered, wishing for her heavy coat, gloves and hat.

"...my money!" That was her kidnapper's voice filtering through the crack of the open door.

"I'll get it to you. I just need a couple of hours." And that was Travis Merrick's.

"Dude! I *kidnapped* her! Now you'll give me my money or you're a dead man, understand?"

Cheyenne pressed shaking fingers to her lips and looked around the area while the two men continued to argue.

"I have a plan to get your money. I just need a little more time. It's all coming together so just—"

Merrick didn't have the money he'd offered for her bounty. No doubt he expected to get a windfall via his scheme to target the city's banking system with his cyber heist. While they were occupied arguing, she would spend her time searching for a phone or a vehicle with keys.

Jack, please be looking for me, please find me.

Snow had started to fall, a light drifting of flakes that melted as soon as they touched the ground that was only just beginning to show through the old layer of snow. That didn't mean things wouldn't change. So stay where someone wanted to kill her or venture out into weather that might also kill her? Which one? She shivered and tucked her cold hands under her armpits while she thought.

Definitely the weather, but which way? She peered through the door and saw them in the kitchen. They moved and finally she could get to the deck steps. She hurried toward them.

More raised voices, then a gunshot sounded and she gasped, spun to see her captor fall to the kitchen floor, hand pressed to his chest, then his eyes closed and his head dropped. Cheyenne squelched a scream and watched. She had a direct line of sight from the French doors through the den and to the front door.

Merrick bent and grabbed the man's legs and hauled him to the front door, then out. The door shut behind him. Cheyenne hurried down the steps while he was preoccupied and found herself in the backyard. Under the deck, at the bottom of the steps, she saw the outside entrance to the basement. She frowned. She hadn't noticed this door from the inside, but she remembered the tall bookcase in the middle of the wall and figured it hid the door.

She tried the knob. Locked. Well, of course. And what was she going to do if it opened? Knock the bookcase over and bring Merrick running? No, but she might have been able to maneuver it and slip around it.

With that no longer an option, she walked up the hill to the front of the home, keeping an eye out for Merrick and staying close to the brick wall. At the top, she took a careful glance around the edge and couldn't see anything thanks to the Suburban in the drive. Tempted to see if he left the keys in the car, she hesitated. A sound in the garage next to her sent her scurrying backward. When Merrick didn't come after her, she dared another peek. He was carrying a shovel and walking toward the tree line across the street, his back to her. She swallowed the sudden surge of bile in her throat. He was going to bury her kidnapper.

God, please give Jack and the others wisdom in how to find me. I know they're searching, but they need your direction. I need it, too. Please get me out of here.

Because if she didn't get away now, she was afraid she was next.

Jack sat back and rubbed his eyes. They'd been at this for too long. How would they find her at this rate? *God please—*

"I think I've got something," Daniel said, his jaw tight.

"What?" the chorus of voices echoed through the room and Jack pulled his chair over next to Daniel's while the others hovered around them. "Show us."

"It's when you were questioning Pullman. Watch."

"That woman," Jack said, "she followed Cheyenne into the room to watch the interrogation."

"Yeah." Daniel tapped the woman on the screen. "Her name is Amy Lee. After watching every step Cheyenne took in the station, I went back and watched hers because Cheyenne had the most contact with her. Now, obviously, there aren't any cameras in the observation area, but watch this." He backed up the footage to where Amy was sitting at her desk. She watched Cheyenne and the others walk past. Then rose and pulled an item out of her top desk drawer to drop in her blazer pocket.

"What was that?" Jack asked.

Daniel glanced at him. "I think it was the tracking device. I think she's the one who put it in Cheyenne's purse."

Jack's fingers tightened into fists. "All right. Let's find her."

"I mean, I can't say for sure, but here's kind of what seals it for me." He clicked and the footage rolled forward to where Amy was at the door to the observation room. She paused, held one coffee in her hand and patted her pocket with the other.

"Like she's reassuring herself that it's there," Jenna said, her voice low.

Jack stood. "Let's go ask her."

"I'll call ahead and make sure she's in the office."

"If she's not, then we'll find her," Jack said.

"If she is, I'll tell them to ensure she stays there."

Jack, Daniel and the dogs walked outside to find the snow falling. All he could do was continue to pray for Cheyenne, that she was warm and not scared. He had a feeling that wasn't the case, though. Emotion clogged his throat for a moment and it was all he could do not to take a swing at something.

"We're going to find her," Daniel said, his voice low, eyes hard and determined.

"I know." But would they find her in time? *God, please lead us to her.*

They finally arrived at the station and Jack checked his phone. "They're in the conference room."

"Not an interrogation room? Interesting."

"This is just an information-finding mission."

"I know. It's just if she is the one who planted the tracker, then the interrogation room would be a lot more intimidating."

"For the average person, maybe. I'm not sure about her."

Daniel shrugged and they walked down the hallway to the conference room. When they entered, Amy was sitting in one of the chairs, her hands clutching the armrests. Her face was pale and she looked almost ill.

"Hi, Amy," Jack said.

"Hi." She cleared her throat. "You wanted to talk to me?"

"We do. Is it all right if I just cut to the chase and be blunt?"

"Of course."

"Someone put a tracker in Cheyenne Chen's purse the other day," Jack said, "and the only person we can come up with who might have done that is you."

She gasped and her eyes widened, but she didn't look away. "Why would you say that?"

Jack leaned in and held her gaze. "Because you had opportunity and we have security footage of you taking it out of your desk before you walked over to fix a cup of coffee that you took into the observation room for Cheyenne. Now, we know you did this—" okay, he might be pushing it with that statement, but he wanted to see what fell over with the shove "—and we want to know who asked you—or paid you—to do it."

Tears welled in her eyes and spilled down her cheeks. Bingo.

Jack passed her the ever-present tissue box.

She took one and dabbed at the moisture then sniffed. "Okay, yeah. When I came into work this morning, there was an envelope on my desk and it had that tracker in it. It said if I wanted to earn two thousand bucks, I'd find a way to put it on Cheyenne Chen." She closed her eyes. "I know I shouldn't have done it, it's just I'm so strapped for money right now and it seemed harmless enough."

Jack slammed a fist on the table. "The guy kidnapped her!"

Amy's face went white. "I'm sorry," she whispered. "I didn't know he was going to hurt her."

"He smoked us out of one safe house and snatched her from another," Daniel said with a warning look at Jack.

Jack worked to get his emotions under control and cleared his throat. "What did you think he was going to do?"

She shook her head. "I didn't think. I just... I don't know! The note said he just wanted to keep up with her, she had something that was his and he needed to get it back without her being around."

"And that didn't raise a red flag? You didn't connect the dots when you learned she was almost run off the road and then the guy in the interrogation room admitted she had a bounty on her head?"

She rubbed her eyes. "Of course I did. But I didn't know how to fix the situation without getting myself in trouble and admitting how stupid I'd been. I'd already dropped it in her purse by the time I realized what was going on."

"Well, if you'd just said something, you would have been in a lot less trouble than you are now."

"So, what now?" she asked, her voice shaky.

"You better hope we find her before it's too late."

TEN

Cheyenne stood next to the brick wall and shivered. She was beyond cold. Merrick was still down by the tree line digging and she figured he'd be occupied for a little while since the ground was probably real close to frozen. But he was making progress so time was ticking down for her. The snow was falling harder and if she struck out for the woods, all Merrick would have to do was follow her footprints in the fresh white powder. Unless the falling snow covered them up. But was it falling fast enough?

Another shiver shuddered through her.

She'd been outside for the past twenty minutes and desperately needed to get warm. There was no way she would survive if she headed for the woods. She'd be frozen solid by morning. She had to get creative because if Merrick caught her, she might be warm, but she'd be dead, too. Which meant she'd still be cold.

When she almost laughed at the morbid thought, she bit her lip. She was losing it.

With that lovely image in mind, she decided the best course of action was to see if there were keys in the Suburban. If not, she'd get back in the house and find a place to hide while Merrick was busy digging the grave. She had no idea if that would work or not, but she was out of options. Keeping an eye on Merrick who had his back to her, she crept up to the Suburban and looked in the window. No keys to see. Tears gathered and she blinked them away. She wouldn't cry. Crying would simply keep her from what she needed to do.

She tried the door.

Unlocked. But that wouldn't help her unless she could start the vehicle.

She left the vehicle door cracked, not wanting to make any noise shutting it. There were no houses in sight, but it just occurred to her that this home sat on a main road. There should be street signs. Maybe she would recognize one. Being careful to stay out of Merrick's line of sight, she hurried across the open area and into the tree line following the road. The same tree line that would hide her kidnapper's grave once Merrick finished digging it.

The cold seeped deep into her bones and her legs grew heavy. But just ahead she thought she caught sight of a street sign. Yes! Conner Street. She didn't know it but now she had a name. So, how to tell someone? An idea flickered in the back of her mind while an airplane flew low overhead, the roar loud in her ears. She couldn't help but wish she was on that flight.

Her teeth chattered and the wind whipped under her hair to chill the back of her neck. She couldn't stay out here. There was only one thing to do. She forced her leaden legs to move and stumbled her way back to the house. Merrick was still trying to dig a hole. As much as she despised the man who'd taken her and put her in this situation, she couldn't help feeling slightly sorry for him. He'd had no idea who Merrick was or what the man was capable of. She'd tried to warn him...

Cheyenne hurried back down the side of the house to the basement and tried the three windows. To her shock, one actually slid open. She crawled through and shut it behind her, realizing she was in the room with the locked door she'd found earlier. She rubbed her arms, noting it was warmer in here, but not by much. She looked around. Electronics were everywhere. Piled on the desk and on all of the shelves that lined the walls from floor to ceiling.

"Okay, then," she whispered, "things might be looking up."

The room was bright enough with the daylight filtering in from outside so she didn't risk turning on the overhead light.

She started with the desk and found an old typewriter, a telephone from the '60s that was dead, of course, and no cord to even try to hook it up. She kept searching and came up with an old cassette player, a VHS player, a Polaroid camera and other items a lot of people her age wouldn't recognize. But with her love of all things electronic, she'd studied them all. And Christmas decorations. Ornaments and stockings, a Christmas tree with the lights still on it in the corner.

Cheyenne ignored all of that and pulled the cover from one of the bulky devices. A gasp slipped from her.

A HAM radio.

"Oh, thank you, Lord, please let it work." If she could get a message out, she could sit tight until rescue came.

With one eye on the window and an ear toward the locked door, she examined the thing. The metal casing showed signs of wear with paint chipped and a dent in the side, but at the moment it was one of the most beautiful items she'd ever seen. The face was made up of knobs and dials, but all held their original labels. It looked to be in really good shape. The microphone was attached, the coiled cable neatly wound and sitting on the table.

But the big question was whether or not it would power on.

She found the antenna wire and noticed it had been secured to the wall and disappeared into the ceiling. Holding her breath, she flipped the power switch and it hummed to life. The display screen glowed amber with the frequency dialed in to something she didn't recognize. She tuned it right to 146.520 MHz, an emergency channel often monitored by amateur users. It was her best hope at having someone hear her.

She held the microphone near her lips with one hand and with the other pressed the push-to-talk button. "Mayday, Mayday, this is Cheyenne Chen and I've been kidnapped. I'm not sure of my location but if someone can contact the Plains City, South Dakota, Police Department, they'll know what to do."

She let go of the button and waited, heart in her throat. Movement outside the window snagged her attention and she hurried to look out. Merrick was coming back inside. He'd be looking for her soon.

She rushed back to the radio and tried again. "Mayday, Mayday, please! This is Cheyenne Chen and I've been kidnapped. Contact the Plains City, South Dakota, Police Department and they'll know what to do. Please respond. Over."

Static crackled. "Copy...signal's weak."

Cheyenne repeated her plea once more. "I'm in a house with a basement. The road name is Conner Street." She thought about the low-flying plane. "I may be near an airport." She said it once more.

"Copy...airport...street..."

The door rattled and her heart bottomed out. So much for sitting tight. Her only escape was back into the bitter cold. Moving fast, she shut off the radio, pulled the cover over it, then slipped back out the window. She closed the window, but through the glass she saw the door open. She dropped to the snow-covered ground.

Jack and the others sat around the table. He had his head in his hands, trying to think while he prayed, asking God for some divine intervention. The others had tried tracking her from the safe house, but the K-9s had come up empty. He shifted and pain shot through his leg. He ignored it and simply moved to a more comfortable position. It hit him that he didn't even care about his leg at the moment. All he cared about was bringing Cheyenne home safely and in one piece. His phone rang and he snapped it up to his ear. "Donodio."

"Ross here. Just got a call from a HAM radio operator saying they had a Mayday message over the airwaves on that channel a lot of amateurs monitor. Someone claiming to be Cheyenne Chen, that she's been kidnapped and they were to contact us."

Jack's pulse jumped. "They say where she is?"

His questions prompted looks from the others. He put the captain on the speakerphone.

"No, but I've got someone working on tracing it. Said he thought she said something about an airport and a street named Donner or Tanner. Said he couldn't hear real clear."

Jack glanced around. "Let's find that out. Now. Call Merrick's brother, Jed, and see if he can give us a location based on that information."

"Good idea," Daniel said. He pulled his phone out.

Hold on, Cheyenne, we're coming. Please, Lord, let us get there in time.

ELEVEN

Cheyenne waited. When Merrick had walked into the room, he'd let out a yell that had rattled the windowpane. He couldn't find her and he was furious. She intended to keep it that way. Once he came up empty with a search of the house, he'd start—

A crash from inside stilled her. She was hidden around the side of the home behind a large bush, but had positioned herself so she could watch the basement door. It didn't take long. The door slammed open just as she'd expected it would. "Cheyenne Chen! There's nowhere to go out here! I'll find you!"

She glanced at the snow. It has covered her tracks for the most part, but she'd been careful not to leave any. She'd walked along the edge of the house, on ground that was still bare, but the snow was falling harder and would cover it soon. The shivers had set in again, but she could ignore them for now. He would be walking around the perimeter, looking for her. She just prayed he went right, not left.

"Cheyenne!"

He went left.

Oh, no.

She only had a few seconds to get around the corner so she darted from the bush and raced up the short side of the ranch home while he stomped the length of the longer side. She bolted around, staying between the bushes and the house, grateful they were trimmed away from the side, not wanting to leave prints.

"Cheyenne! You have to pay for what you did!"

She reached the front door, pulled it open and slipped inside, shutting it behind her. She almost locked it, then stopped. If he couldn't get in, he'd know for sure she was inside. She could only pray the dirty snow on the porch disguised her new prints. She stepped out of her tennis shoes and, carrying them in one hand, in socked feet, hurried to the basement door that was now open and still hanging by one hinge. Her only hope was the radio. She had to try one more time. She scrambled down the stairs straight to the room with the radio where she shut the door behind her, ripped the cover off the radio and flipped the power on. It was still tuned to the right frequency. "Mayday. Mayday. Are you still there? Over."

"Affirmative. Are you Cheyenne Chen. Over."

"Yes. I'm at—"

The door opened and she spun to see Merrick holding a gun on her, a hard cold smile on his face. "Say another word and I'll end this now."

She stayed silent and he walked toward her. She dropped the mic and backed up. Merrick stopped next to the radio and pulled the plug. "Now, we get to have a chat before you die."

Cheyenne let out a slow breath while she struggled for another plan. How had he—

"Thought you were pretty smart, huh?" he asked, his expression taunting. "Thought your little game of cat and mouse was keeping you out of my grasp?"

Still, she said nothing.

"Thought you could outsmart me, didn't you? When will you learn? I'm the genius here. Saw you trying to sneak around the corner of the house and knew I had you. When I couldn't find any prints or any sign of you, I decided you slipped back inside the house so you could get down here. The only piece of communication around this place is that radio. Looks like I guessed right."

"Where are all your computers?" The question popped out before she could stop it.

He snorted. "Not where you could find them, that's for sure. You think you're so smart. Well, this time I'm the smarter one. You'll be dead and your reputation in ruins."

"It's not enough for me to die, you want to completely ruin me. Make it look like all of this is on me."

"Exactly." He shot a disgusted glance at the radio. "Forgot that was there until I thought I heard you talking on it. Then I walked in to find the room empty. But the window was unlocked. Figured you got out that way." He nodded to the window.

"It was unlocked to begin with. It's how I got *in*."

He frowned. "Huh. Whatever." He waved the gun. "Come on, let's go."

"Where?"

He backed up and the gun never wavered. Cheyenne refused to show her fear and contemplated the best self-defense moves but she was fully aware he was a trained martial arts expert. Anything she tried he'd be able to deflect. There was no way she'd be able to beat him in hand-to-hand combat. So she'd simply have to outsmart him. That strategy hadn't worked so well on the many who'd snatched her from the safe house, but this time it would have to. It was her only chance.

She couldn't deny she was terrified, but she was also angry. She'd put him away once; she'd figure out how to do it again.

She let him guide her out of the room. "Who was the guy who kidnapped me?"

"Bart Isaacs. Bounty hunter out of Arkansas. Seemed like he had some good sense. Followed the directions and only called when he had you."

"Okay. But how did he find me?"

"No idea and don't care. Now up."

He'd led her to the steps. She looked up. He wanted her to go first. That might work in her favor. She placed her foot on the bottom step and started up while he stayed two steps behind her.

A plan formed as she climbed, but she'd have to act quick and she'd only get one shot. Her pulse sped up, but it was now or never. She looked back, noted the location of the weapon. And his head. "Go!" As though obeying, she turned back to face the door, noticed it had been repaired, the hinges now repinned. But if he wanted her to go up, it was probably unlocked.

Two steps from the top, she gripped the rail on her right with her left hand and spun, kicking out. Her foot connected with the gun and it flew from his grip. He gave a strangled yell and, still holding the rail, she shot another kick to his head, catching him in the face. He fell backward and thudded down the steps. His screams of rage and pain followed her through the door that she slammed behind her, then twisted the deadbolt with a click.

But he could still get out and he had the gun down there with him. She ran out the front door just as a black SUV pulled to the curb.

Jack and Beau spilled out of the vehicle, then Jenna and Augie from another, and Daniel and Dakota. She ran to Jack while tears streamed down her cheeks. "He's not contained," she yelled. "He's got a gun. He'll probably come out of the basement door."

Jack shoved her toward the SUV, but she shook him off. "He's mine, Jack."

He paused and nodded, then followed her and the others around the side of the house and down the hill to see the basement door open and Travis Merrick step through it. He lifted his weapon, eyes wild. "You're dead, Cheyenne Chen!"

A shot rang out and Merrick dropped. A SWAT team member had done the job.

Officers rushed him and Jack pulled Cheyenne into his arms as though he'd never let her go. And she was just fine with that.

Jack had never been so glad to hold someone in his arms and he might just keep her there for infinity. "You terrified me," he murmured into her left ear.

They were seated in the back of the ambulance with the heat

running while Daniel, Jenna and Captain Ross took care of the details. Travis Merrick was dead and Cheyenne was safe. She was *safe*. He had to repeat it over and over in his head before he could start to believe it.

"Trust me, there was plenty of terror going on over here, too," she muttered.

He tightened his grip. Just enough to reassure himself that she was really there, not hard enough to hurt. Beau, who'd been stretched out by the door, raised his head, then crawled over to wedge it between them. Cheyenne laughed and scratched his ears. He licked her face.

Jack pushed the dog away with a firm, "Settle." Beau slunk back to his spot by the door and looked at him with reproachful eyes. He sighed and determined to give the dog an extra treat when they finally got home. In the meantime, he held Cheyenne at arm's length to look her in the eyes. "I thought I'd lost you."

"That makes two of us," she whispered. "How did you find me?"

"The HAM operator called us, gave us the name of a street—well, sort of. He got it wrong, but we figured it out. He also said you thought you were near an airport so that helped a lot."

"He heard that?"

"Yeah. Said that was about all he heard other than the *Mayday* words."

She shook her head. "Where are we? How far is the airport?"

"About five miles."

"I should have risked it," she whispered. "I just didn't know where I was and with the cold and the snow—" She tightened the blanket around her and Jack pulled her back to him. "I was scared to risk it," she said.

"It's okay, Cheyenne. You're safe now and that's all that matters."

The paramedic cleared her throat and he shot her a glare. She pursed her lips like she wanted to argue, but stepped back. "Five more minutes, then we roll, okay?"

He nodded, then turned back to Cheyenne just as Daniel walked up. "How are you?" He placed a hand on her shoulder and Jack had to refrain from knocking it off. They were friends, nothing more.

He relaxed. Daniel raised a brow at him and smiled.

But removed his hand.

Cheyenne nodded and took a sip of the hot coffee someone had found and pushed into her hands. "I'm all right. You got here just in time, though. I don't know what I would have done if I'd had to fight to get away from him again." She shuddered and Jack wished the guy was alive so he could punch him.

"Go away," Jack told Daniel, his tone mild. "And get me a few more minutes before they decide they need to haul her to the hospital, pretty please?"

"I don't need to go to the hospital," Cheyenne said.

"He hit you in the head."

"But he didn't knock me out. It's okay. *I'm* okay. Really."

Captain Ross walked over and Jack suppressed a groan. He'd never get any time with her at this rate. "You're going to the hospital, Chen, and that's an order."

She bit her lip and nodded. "Yes, sir. I guess I'm going to the hospital."

The paramedic came back and crossed her arms. Jack knew when he was beat. "Beau and I'll be right behind you."

TWELVE

It didn't take long for the doctor to declare Cheyenne just fine and sign off on her discharge. "Someone will be here shortly to do the paperwork," the woman said.

Cheyenne nodded. "Thank you."

The doctor left and Beau rose from his spot by the sink to walk over and rest his snout on Cheyenne's knee. His dark eyes said he'd been concerned, too, and was glad she was safe. She stroked her fingers through his soft fur, grateful for his soothing presence. Jack moved to sit beside her and took her hand. "I haven't called your parents because I wasn't sure you wanted me to. From the little you said about it, I didn't get that you were very close."

"We're not, but we're not estranged, either. I don't need to fill them in on any of this. If the news reaches them, then I'll explain, but for now, I don't want to tell them."

"Okay, I can respect that." A pause. "What are you doing for Christmas? I know you usually go home. Are you still planning on doing that?"

"No," she said, "I'm planning on *staying* home this year. This place has become my home. Mom and Dad are going back to China to visit some relative I didn't even know existed."

"So you'll be here for Christmas." A smiled curved his lips. "Excellent. Now, are you up to finishing our conversation?"

She took a deep breath. Was she? "More than ready. But first, please, I have a few more questions."

"Sure."

"How did Merrick keep tracking us to the different safe houses?"

"Amy Lee put a tracker in your purse when you were at the station the night Pullman broke into your house."

"Oh. Oh, wow."

"I know. She's facing some serious charges, including accessory to kidnapping."

"I'm just...stunned. I never would have connected her to that. So, the guy in the white van, the person who tried to smoke us out and all of that was the man who snatched me."

"Yep. I got a text a little while ago and the coroner recovered his body. He had a few priors, was mixed up with some pretty bad dudes."

"He said he was. And that even knowing I might be killed, he still had to go through with it. So sad."

"There are a lot of lessons to be learned through all of this. Not the least of which is about life choices and the paths we choose to follow. And the whole consequences-slash-rewards thing." He cleared his throat. "Which leads me full circle back to the car conversation."

And just like that, her pulse skyrocketed once more.

"I want to clear the air so to speak," he said. "In the car, we talked about a few things. You told me a bit about how you felt and now it's my turn to do the same."

Cheyenne held her breath.

"I finally realized when I might lose you that I never really had you," he said. "But I definitely didn't want to lose you—or the possibility of a future with you in it." Her heart started that weird pounding it did whenever Jack talked like that to her. Then his eyes darkened. He rubbed a hand over his mouth, curled his fingers into a fist and stood to pace to the window.

She bit her lip and the warm fuzzies cooled. "Jack?"

He was silent a moment longer before he turned to look at her. "I haven't told anyone, but the bullet I took almost a year ago is lodged in a precarious place in my leg right up against the bone. It still causes me occasional pain depending on how I move. Initially, when I was cleared for duty, all looked fine. Then the bullet moved. My most recent check-up and x-ray showed some concern. It's possible if it continues to move, it could cause major problems. To the point that they might have to rescind my fit for duty status and stick me back on a desk job. As time goes on, it's possible I could even lose my leg."

She gasped. "Oh, Jack, how awful. I'm so sorry." Then she frowned. "But why didn't they just take it out? And you're back on active duty. You're running and…and very active and…how is it that okay?"

He shrugged when she finally snapped her lips shut. "The bullet is well and truly stuck. Taking it out was ruled more dangerous than leaving it in. And, right now, while it gives me pain in certain positions, I'm fine. Full range of motion, I can run, chase bad guys, and so on. It's just the unknown. Will it move or will it not?" A sigh slipped from him.

"No one knows what the future holds. And I know it's really easy to say the key is trusting God when there's no threat that I may lose my leg, but when I was in that basement and thought I might really not make it out—" she shuddered and tried not to let the fear grab hold again "—I had no choice but to trust that God would either save me—or not, but it was up to me to fight for what I wanted. And that was my freedom—and you. I wanted to be able to tell you how much I cared about you. I wanted to live more than just about anything." Her voice trailed to a whisper and he strode to her to pull her into a tight hug.

"I wanted that just about more than anything, too," he said. "And in my head, I know you're right. God has the ultimate say in what happens, but when the doctor told me that, I…" He shrugged and let her go to return to the window. "As much as

I was falling for you at the time, I didn't want to bring anyone else into my drama."

"It's not drama. It's... Well, I don't know what it is, but it's not drama." She hesitated, then stood to walk over to him. She slid her arms around his waist and he raised his hands to cup her shoulders. She looked up. "You were falling for me?"

His lips quirked into a small smile. "Yeah."

"Good. Because I was falling for you, too." She sighed and turned serious. "I'm tired of living in fear, tired of being afraid of taking risks," she whispered. "I want to be there for you. To support you and care for you." His gaze filled with a longing that sparked hope in her heart. "I love you, Jack. I have for a long time."

A tear spilled over and slid down his cheek and he wiped it away, then cleared his throat. "I've wanted to hear those words for a while now. I've wanted to say them, too. I just..."

"I know. I get it. I grew up bullied, never feeling like I belonged until I became a part of the DGTF and when I started having feelings for you...it terrified me."

He raised a brow. "Why?"

"What if something went wrong and we broke up? Would I have to break up with all my friends—people who've become my family—too? I was afraid to risk it."

"And now?"

She stood on tiptoe and placed her lips on his. He pulled her to him and kissed her back like it was something he'd been dreaming of for a very long time. Cheyenne put her heart into the connection, willing him to feel, to trust, to love. And he did. When he finally lifted his head, his eyes smoked with emotion and passion. "Does that answer your question?" she asked.

"What question?"

She giggled. "The question you asked me before I kissed you."

"Oh, *and now*?"

"Yeah. And now. Now, I've discovered real things to be afraid of. And it's not us. You're—*we're*—worth the risk."

He leaned his forehead against hers and closed his eyes. When he opened them, he locked them onto hers. "I don't know what's going to happen with my leg."

"I don't know, either, but God does and I think the three of us make a pretty awesome team."

He kissed her again and Cheyenne leaned into it until the door opened. And even then, Jack didn't seem like he was in a hurry to let her go.

"Well, well," Jenna said, "what do we have here?"

Beau barked and wiggled between them. Cheyenne laughed and rubbed his head while Jack chuckled.

Daniel stepped inside minus Dakota, but he held Joy in his arms and Aurora was with him.

As the others filed in, one by one, the room was almost filled to bursting. "How many hospital rules are you guys breaking right now?" Cheyenne asked, not one bit disturbed by the fact.

"A lot," Daniel said. "Which means we probably need to disappear, but we wanted you to know that we're here for you."

She couldn't speak through the lump in her throat and Jack slid an arm around her shoulders as though he knew exactly what her problem was. Finally, she cleared the lump and swiped at a few stray tears. "Thank you," she whispered. "I love you all."

"And we love you," Jenna said.

Beau barked again and everyone laughed.

The door opened and a nurse stood there, papers in hand. "Um, a few of you probably need to leave."

Daniel nodded. "We're headed out now. Sorry about the intrusion. We just had to show our support and love."

"I'm all about that, personally. Professionally? Out, please."

They filed out and Cheyenne curled into Jack's side, breathing in the scent of him, hardly believing that her dreams were coming true. *Thank you, God, so very much. For everything.*

At the door, Daniel turned back and smiled and motioned to the two of them. "By the way, this? It's about time."

Beau barked his agreement and Cheyenne and Jack laughed.

And as the door closed behind Daniel, Cheyenne turned to Jack. "I'm in full agreement with them all," she said.

And he kissed her again. She took that to mean the agreement was unanimous.

* * * * *

*If you enjoyed Cheyenne and Jack's story,
don't miss Lorelai's story next!*

*And check out the rest of the
Dakota K-9 Unit series!*

Chasing a Kidnapper
by Laura Scott, April 2025

Deadly Badlands Pursuit
by Sharee Stover, May 2025

Standing Watch
by Terri Reed, June 2025

Cold Case Peril
by Maggie K. Black, July 2025

Tracing Killer Evidence
by Jodie Bailey, August 2025

Threat of Revenge
by Jessica R. Patch, September 2025

Double Protection Duty
by Sharon Dunn, October 2025

Final Showdown
by Valerie Hansen, November 2025

Christmas K-9 Patrol
by Lynette Eason and Lenora Worth, December 2025

*Available only from Love Inspired Suspense.
Discover more at LoveInspired.com.*

Dear Reader,

Thank you for coming along on this rollercoaster ride of a journey with Cheyenne and Jack. As you may have noticed, this is a story of courage, resilience, and learning to trust—not just in each other but in God's plan, even when the path ahead seemed uncertain.

Cheyenne's brilliance and independence made her an incredible force to reckon with, but like so many of us, she sometimes struggled to let others in. Jack, on the other hand, is fiercely protective and driven by a sense of justice, yet his past has left him wary of vulnerability as well. Together, they faced not only the external threats of a high-stakes situation but also the internal battles of learning to trust again.

As I wrote their story, I was reminded of the truth in Joshua 1:9. This verse reflects the journey Cheyenne and Jack take as they learn to fight back even when they're afraid—to trust that God has their back and is in the trenches with them fighting alongside them. I hope their journey inspires you to reflect on your own moments of uncertainty or fear and reminds you that God always has a plan even when we can't see it or the future looks bleak. Whether you're facing challenges in your personal life, relationships, or faith, know that God is with you every step of the way and you don't have to be afraid of the outcome.

Thank you for spending your time with these characters and for joining me on this adventure. If you enjoyed the story, I'd love to hear from you. You can find me at www.lynetteeason.com, where you can sign up for my monthly newsletter. I'm also on Facebook at www.facebook.com/lynette.eason and X at @lynetteeason. I look forward to hearing what you think about the story.

God Bless,
Lynette Eason

DANGEROUS HOLIDAY MANHUNT

Lenora Worth

To the war dogs and K-9 heroes
that help our human military and law enforcement
agencies every day.

You are truly man's best friend.
(And woman's best friend, too!)

For God hath not given us the spirit of fear;
but of power, and of love, and of a sound mind.
—*2 Timothy* 1:7

ONE

US Marshal Lorelai Danvers opened the back of her unmarked SUV and signaled. "Come, Bixby," she said, admiring the Australian shepherd's fur and wishing she could stay as warm as her partner. The mix of thick black, tan and white fur demanded a lot of maintenance. She wouldn't have it any other way. A trained K-9 officer, Bixby had been her tracking partner for five years now.

After she'd hooked a leash to Bixby's official K-9 vest, she leaned down and met his dark gaze, nose to nose. "Don't go herding through the snow on me now, okay? We've got business here and you don't have on your snow boots."

Here being the Triple C Ranch. She hoped she'd be allowed into the house. A winding road fenced on both sides led up to the massive house made of glass, beams and stone. Surrounded by the snow-covered plains and rocky foothills of South Dakota, the Triple C was a few miles out from Badlands National Park. Brutal country, but after a few weeks of winter, Lorelai's southern bones were slowly adjusting. She had a lot of parkas, puffer coats and sweaters, and she had a closet full of boots.

She studied the symmetric angles of the house and admired the large Christmas tree sparkling with glittering white lights through the floor-to-ceiling windows of the huge den, reminding her of the season and the few days left before Christmas. Right now, her mind wasn't on the holidays.

She hoped the latest tip she'd received from a park ranger would help her finally bring in a man wanted for an unsolved murder six months ago. After digging through files and reports, and talking to eyewitnesses, they'd finally had enough evidence to bring in Booker Gleason. She hadn't been in on the raid in North Dakota last week, but she'd been notified that Gleason had escaped while being transferred, and he'd been at-large since. Two days ago, he'd been spotted just outside the park. The park ranger had identified a man walking on the highway near the Triple C's open gate. He'd called it in right away because all the rangers were aware that Gleason could be hiding out in the area.

Earlier in the year, Lorelai had gone after leads regarding Gleason across the Dakotas until she'd been assigned to another case.

After a bad breakup a year ago, she'd asked to be transferred from Savannah, and the district of South Dakota had an opening. Not exactly her first choice but she took it, liking the challenge. Searching for Booker Gleason had been one of her first assignments here, until she'd been brought in four months ago to replace another officer on the Dakota Gun Task Force. Now that the DGTF had brought down the gun traffickers they'd chased all year, things had settled down to her usual routine. With Gleason still at-large, she'd asked to be put back on the hunt.

When she'd gotten the tip on Gleason, followed by a report of a prowler near the ranch, she got back to business and found a juicy little side-note. Booker Gleason had once worked on this ranch.

During the holiday downtime, she planned to catch this killer. Lorelai didn't like fugitives and she had a reputation of always getting her man. While she'd given up on a good man to spend her life with because her overbearing parents thought they needed to pick that man, which never worked, she thrived on bringing in bad men. If Gleason had been laying low in or near the Badlands National Park, she'd put the holidays on hold and get back to work finding him. When the park ranger had mentioned the Corbin Cattle Company, known as the Triple C Ranch, Lorelai had ignored all the warnings about the ornery owner who didn't like people on his property. Gleason might be returning to a place he knew, possibly to hide out.

She had a good reason to be here.

If Booker Gleason had so much as sneezed on this vast acreage, she and Bixby would know it and they'd find him.

Now she waited for the man of the house to open the door and talk to her. Unable to reach him by phone, she'd decided to show up in person.

She liked in-person discussions better anyway, and she hoped the infamous Drake Corbin would talk to her face-to-face.

That problem was soon solved.

The door slammed open and before she could get a boot on the first stone step leading up to the long porch, she found a tall well-built man with a head of salt-and-pepper hair holding a Remington pointed at her forehead.

Keeping the rifle and his gaze on her, he asked in a gravelly voice, "Who are you and what are you doing on my land?"

Lorelai glanced from the rifle to the man, then flipped out her badge. "Deputy US Marshal Lorelai Danvers. I came to see you, Mr. Corbin, because I heard about a prowler nearby here last night. Possibly a wanted fugitive. I need to ask you a few questions."

"Lady," he said with a handsome smirk while his onyx gaze narrowed toward her gold-star badge, "I have all kinds of prowler coming onto my land and I know how to handle them without a US marshal's help."

Cold and tired, Lorelai sighed with impatience and pushed the gun barrel to the left, surprising the man holding it. "Do you know how to handle a killer who goes by the name of Booker Gleason?"

He dropped the gun and stared at her, really looking at her this time, his eyes wide with shock and anger, and an emotion she recognized well enough—regret.

Lowering the rifle, he growled, "Maybe you'd better come inside and explain yourself."

"My partner, Bixby, comes with me," she replied as she passed the heavy wooden door carved with intricate Pasque motifs—South Dokata's state flower. "Hope that's not a problem."

Drake Corbin's forehead furrowed as he studied her and huffed, "I like dogs. Worrisome women, not so much."

And yet, he let her inside the house.

Drake focused on the pretty intruder who'd managed to elbow her way into his home. Just what he needed on a snowy December night. Trouble. Not that he minded a woman showing up out of the blue, but this one was an officer of the law and had mentioned a name he'd tried to wipe out of his memory. Booker Gleason was not welcome here.

Drake studied her, trying to decide if this was a bad joke. Almost as tall as him, she had a cute head of blond hair stopping just short of her ears, bringing attention to her green eyes. She wore faded jeans, butter-colored cowgirl boots that looked aged and comfortable, and the heaviest bright blue hooded puffer coat he'd ever seen.

He watched as she pushed at her hair, knocking shaggy bangs to one side before she slipped out of the long coat. He motioned and she handed the coat to him. Drake placed it across one of the two black leather couches centered across from the big fireplace. She had on a deep blue wool sweater that almost swallowed her slim figure.

Staring at the US marshal, he said, "So, you must need information bad if you came out on a night like this. You do know this storm isn't going to let up, don't you?"

Maybe she'd leave and he'd check on this intruder himself.

Her green-eyed frown lasered in on him. "Storms don't concern me. Fugitives do."

Fugitives. His heart did a leap, warning him that she meant

business. One of his men had found an abandoned campsite up near the road in a thicket of trees. Drake had shrugged it off since people came and went around here a lot, some of them on foot and homeless.

"Booker Gleason is a fugitive from the law?"

Drake hadn't seen the man in years and he sure didn't want to find Gleason on his land. Then again, people went missing around here, too. It would be easy to make that happen with a man he'd hated for most of his life. Remembering his wife and how he'd made a promise to her, he'd refrained from murder and violence. If her evil half-brother had returned, well, that changed things.

"Has anyone been hanging around on your land, Mr. Corbin?"

Feisty. Drake wouldn't dare call her that out loud. The woman looked like she could handle both a storm and a fugitive.

She waited, her gaze centered on him.

"One of my men reported a campfire up by the road."

"Then we need to discuss this a bit more."

"Okay." He gave in because she intrigued him, not to mention he needed to hear how she'd tracked Booker Gleason to this ranch. Keeping things light in case he didn't like what she had to tell him, he said, "We need to talk. I've had a long day herding cattle and making sure my livestock are safe from this upcoming storm. I'm hungry and I have coffee or hot chocolate."

"I'm all in for coffee," she said, her eyes lighting up. "Black."

"Black it is," he replied, liking her bluntness. Trying to keep things light while his heart pounded with a heavy beat, he smiled. "My chef left some big homemade cookies in the kitchen. Follow me and we'll get you some food."

"I didn't come here to eat." Her gaze flashed over the big den and the black wrought iron staircase. "But I can't resist a good cookie." Then she asked, "You have a chef?"

"More like a drill sergeant," he replied. "Rena's my sister. She'd been here with me for twenty years." He stopped, not wanting to share his past. "She's only a few years older than me and she takes care of things around the house."

He didn't want to think of all those years or the man she'd come looking for, so he focused on the problem at hand. Not what he'd been expecting on this snowy December night. Especially her telling him Booker Gleason could be snooping around. Drake had made it clear long ago that he'd better not show his face here again.

"Hmm, I reckon that explains why you don't like worrisome women."

He actually chuckled, her remark bringing him back to the here and now. "You're not winning points."

Her narrowed gaze made her look even cuter. "I'm not trying to win points. I need answers."

"C'mon, then." Drake had planned to have a quiet night, maybe reading a book or watching an old movie. He'd never thought he'd hear Gleason might be back and roaming around on his property. And he couldn't tell the marshal he'd prefer to take care of the situation himself.

He took her up the open hallway that ran through the house and into the big kitchen he rarely used. "Have a seat at the bar there."

Lorelai glanced around and whistled, causing both Drake and her K-9 to lift their ears. "Will you be able to find me? That's a big counter you got there."

"It's a big house." He shrugged and poured coffee into two chunky mugs, then opened the massive industrial-size refrigerator and found the sliced turkey and cheese tray Rena had left before she retired to her room. Placing the platter on the island, he said, "I'm having a late supper. You can join me."

She nabbed a square of Gruyère and a thick slice of turkey.

"You're not as mean as I've heard," she said, her gaze a blank page. "But you are good at stalling."

Handing her a linen napkin, he countered, "I'm sure you've heard a lot of things about me, Marshal. Right now, I want to hear about this fugitive you're tracking. You think he's hiding out on my land?"

"Lorelai," she replied. "Call me Lorelai."

He liked that name, so he nodded and watched as she broke off a stem of grapes from the platter and tore into them.

After she took a sip of coffee, she pulled out a mug shot and handed it over to where he stood across from her. "Do you know this man? Killed a man in North Dakota a few months back, and he has several prior arrests—petty theft, drunk and disorderly, aggravated assault, attacking coworkers, little things like that. My colleague finally located him last week, but he escaped while in transit to a prison near the southern border of North Dakota. Holds a grudge from what I've learned."

Drake liked her southern accent, but not her reason for being here. "Lot of people hold grudges. That's not a crime." He'd be in jail himself if that was the case.

He knew this man and yes, Booker Gleason had a big-time grudge against Drake. He glanced out into the night and then turned back to the woman waiting for him to explain, a deep exhaustion pushing at his soul.

Lorelai Danvers dropped the oatmeal cookie she'd just grabbed and looked him square in the eye. "It is if that grudge causes you to want to get even by murdering people."

Drake stood holding his mug, the warmth from the coffee soothing against his callused fingers. He took a drink and then set his brew down on the white marble counter that shimmered from Rena's many wipe-downs. Watching the woman sitting across from him, he wondered how much he should tell her. He never liked to reveal his cards too soon with anyone, especially a stranger who happened to be the law. She probably knew all the answers to her questions already and just needed someone to confirm them. She'd bide her time by enjoying these refreshments.

Or maybe she was hungry. He liked a woman with a good appetite.

"Well?" She held his gaze, her green eyes making him miss spring, and also stirring a memory of a woman walking through a meadow. He'd loved once. Only once. He didn't plan to go down that path again. "If you know something about this man, Mr. Corbin, you'd better tell me right now."

Maybe she didn't know everything about Booker's background. Figured that Gleason would fly under the radar.

Her southern drawl danced like a dragonfly over his senses. "Call me Drake," he said. "You're not from around here are you, Miss Lorelai Danvers?"

A flash of aggravation flickered through those green eyes like water rippling across a creek bed. "I'm from Savannah, Georgia, but sidetracking me isn't going to make me leave." Then she burned him with a heated gaze. "And never call me miss again."

"Okay, I'm not sidetracking you but this weather could," he finally said. This storm could get worse and he'd not get that good night's sleep he'd planned. "Now, regarding the man you mentioned, the name is familiar to me. Very familiar."

Her eyes glittered with curiosity. "Now we're getting somewhere? How so?"

Drake opened his mouth to tell her about how Gleason had caused his wife's death. A shot rang out, echoing through the night like a rocket going off. Then another shot shattered glass as the window over the sink crinkled but didn't break open. Drake sprinted around the corner and grabbed her off the high stool, dragging her down to the floor. "Stay down."

Shocked, she stared at him as they crouched behind the kitchen island, then gave her growling dog a signal that quieted the beautiful creature. "Let me up so I can do my job," she said, drawing a Glock 22 out from underneath her long sweater.

Drake watched in amazement as she went tense, her eyes narrowed as she scanned the room. Her K-9 shook with anticipation. Honestly, Drake had been around all kinds of women and this one had impressed him from the get-go. But he wouldn't let the marshal get killed on his account because he couldn't allow that to happen again.

"I can't do that," he said, reaching up a hand to grab the rifle he'd left near the counter. "My property, my protection duty. Someone is shooting at us."

"I know that," she said with a drawling frustration. "And I think we both know who that someone is, don't we?" Shifting away from him, she added, "Let me take care of our visitor and then you can tell me what you should have said before he started shooting at us, okay?"

And with that, she went into action and moved through the house like a sprite, shifting and crouching here and there, her gun steady and her trusty canine following her with a loyal cadence.

Rena appeared on the stairs, calling out. "Drake, are you having target practice?"

"An intruder," he shouted, his gaze on the woman who'd just ran out the door. "Get back to your room. I'll explain later."

Rena shrugged and went back upstairs.

"Hey, wait up," Drake called out the door to Lorelai. "Before you get both of us killed."

Another shot rang out, and this time, a returning shot through the open back door met it head-on. A shot coming from a worrisome woman's fancy gun.

"Well," Drake mumbled as he moved to get her out of the line of fire, "I can't let her leave now. Booker will kill her for sure." And he'd do it just to get even with Drake.

TWO

Lorelai trudged through the growing snow, following the obvious path the shooter had covered, Bixby right along with her. She had snow boots in her SUV, but no time to put them on the K-9 to protect his paws. Bixby specialized in tracking, but this weather would be a test for both of them.

"We won't stay out here long," she whispered to her faithful companion as she searched the area. Cold wet drops of snow landed on her hair and face and clung to her heavy sweater. Shivering, she said, "I won't let your paws freeze, and I don't think I'll be able go too far out in this, anyway."

"No, you sure won't."

She spun around to find Drake right behind her with his trusty rifle. "I need you to come back inside. I can't protect you if you get lost in the snow."

She kept trudging. "In case you haven't noticed, I'm trained to protect myself and apparently, now you."

He sighed. "In case you haven't noticed, I also know how to protect myself and now, you and your working K-9, too. I'm asking nicely for you to come back inside where we can talk and plan our strategy."

She whipped around, slinging snow out in front of her boots. "You have a strategy?"

"I do."

"He's out here now."

"He can't get far in this mess and neither can you. The snow will get heavier overnight. You want to take him in and I want that, too. But he knows this land well enough to survive on it. I can help you do your job and keep both of us alive."

Lorelai lowered her head and stared out into the darkness where snow glistened like a thick white blanket. Out of her element, she wasn't used to someone else calling the shots. "It would be easy to get stuck out there."

"You have no idea. I've been out in this all day long, preparing. I don't want to chase you through a foot of fresh snow. And just so you understand, Booker Gleason won't get far in this, either. He'll find shelter and hunker down."

She didn't want to give in, but in this case what else could she do? She knew it snowed here. She'd become more acclimated once she'd spent a winter here, and she'd been training Bixby to be prepared. Tonight's weather threw her off.

"Is there any way we could search for him, like right now?"

"Several ways," Drake said. "He's hoping we'll do just that."

As if the man they were talking about had been listening in, another round of gunshots hit the silent night with banging echoes. Bixby tensed and growled while Drake and Lorelai crouched near a snow-covered maple tree. Lorelai glanced toward the woods. No bullets reached where they stood. "He's shooting some distance away, and frankly, his aim is not great."

"My point exactly," Drake said. "He knows the lay of this land and obviously, he's been hiding out for a while. If he wants me, he'll return sooner or later. He probably doesn't know you're even here. If he does, he'll think you're a friend of mine. And that means you're collateral damage. Let's get inside and come up with a better plan. He might not be good at shooting, but he won't have to be a great shot to bring one of us down."

She stomped her boots in protest, let out a frustrated sigh and took off past him toward the house. "I'm beginning to hate snow."

"You'll get used to it if you stay here much longer. We don't get storms like this very often and usually they happen after the holiday season. This one came up quick and without much warning, kinda like you and the man you're hunting."

She took the information in and didn't ask where *here* could be—his ranch or the Dakotas in general—and she really wasn't sure about that herself just now.

She marched back toward the looming house and watched lacy snowflakes dancing in the beam of a security light. Everything had become eerily white. Bixby followed, confused about why they weren't in pursuit.

Drake came up behind her. "He won't give up. Good thing you warned me about him."

"I wanted verification that he could be here and well, we got it," she retorted. "I'd be flying into the mist if I tried to find him now, but I sure wish I could track him down."

"Glad you're beginning to see things my way," he replied. "Maybe we can search for him come daylight when I go out to check on my animals. I'm sure you're a capable officer. All training aside, you're dealing with a heartless man who has no scruples. Trust me, I know."

His statement indicated two things to Lorelai. Drake Corbin expected she'd be here in the morning, due to the weather, and he planned to track Booker Gleason himself, with or without her.

"Okay." She allowed him to guide her to the big house and through a side door. She wouldn't leave here without trying, and if that meant she had to bunk down in the corner of this massive house until the weather got better, she'd make it work.

Once they were back inside, he turned off lights, set an alarm and moved through the darkness to stoke the fire. That done, he pointed to a big leather ottoman near the fireplace. "Take off your boots and get your feet warm. Your socks are probably wet."

Before Lorelai grudgingly did as he asked, she checked Bixby's paws, rubbing them and making sure she'd cleaned them as best she could. Bixby stood near the roaring fire, his eyes bright. When she gave him the signal to heel, he settled in place on the oval rope rug that hugged the area near the fireplace, his dark-eyed gaze on a porcelain reindeer surrounded by fake evergreen branches on the mantel. A couple of Christmas cards stood lined up next to the decorations, making Lorelai remember she needed to send her parents the obligatory gift card that they'd probably throw in a drawer somewhere and forget.

"You're giving up, too?" she asked Bixby in a teasing voice, her mind still on alert. Bixby never gave up and neither did she. Had Booker Gleason gotten away? He would know how to survive for a while, she imagined. He probably had some sort of snowmobile to help him get around. Feeling like a rookie although she'd been a deputy for years, she said, "I guess I picked the wrong night to track a fugitive."

"You sure did," Drake said as he brought over two mugs of fresh coffee. "You were spot on, thinking he's here. And that's one step toward your goal of catching him."

"I like your optimistic take on this," she said in a sarcasm-laced voice. "I've read up on his history and I know he worked here long ago. I'd like it if you tell me what you know about this man."

Drake nodded and sat down in a puffy dark leather chair. "Well, since we're stuck here and it's gonna be a long night, I reckon I should do that."

Drake figured she wouldn't let him rest until he confessed the basics of what he knew. He also figured she might be here for days. This storm wasn't playing.

Lorelai kept her bright eyes on him, waiting. He imagined her doing that with a suspect in custody. Intimidation looked good on her and made him realize how serious this situation had become. What could he reveal without telling too many secrets? He had to protect his home and his grown children who would be coming home for Christmas. He hoped. They were safe and away from all of this for now, but he might have to warn them away.

"Booker Gleason is my brother-in-law," he finally said, hating the mention of the man's name.

She didn't even blink. "I had a feeling you knew him better than you'd let on. You being related to Gleason adds a whole new wrinkle to this case. Makes me wonder why I didn't find that in the dossier. But I'm coming up with reasons. Such as you possibly harboring a fugitive. Did you tell him to run out the back, then come around and shoot, making it look like he wanted to target both of us?"

Drake gave her a stone-cold glare. "Don't go there. You've been with me since I opened the door. I can assure you, I want the man off the streets probably more than you do."

"So he's here for what—a holiday visit—or maybe revenge?"

"What do you think?"

"I'm thinking he's hiding out on your property because he wants to get to you, either for your help or to harm you. He's killed before, and if you didn't invite him, he must have showed up for one reason—to take you out. My question is why?"

"I'm thinking the same thing and I can tell you why. He's certainly not here to drink wassail and eat fruit cake. The man hates me as much as I hate him."

Lorelai put down her empty coffee mug. "So what happened with you two?"

Drake braced himself. He didn't like to talk about his history with Booker but she had come here on a mission, so he had no other choice. He'd never lied to the law and he wasn't about to start now. "Well, as you probably know from vetting me, I'm a widower. My wife died from a horse accident twenty years ago." He stopped, remembering that day so clearly, his heart did a fast leap. "Booker Gleason killed her, and it's partly my fault, too."

Lorelai came off her chair and paced in front of the fire. "What are you saying, Drake?"

"We'd been married five years and had a four-year-old son and a baby daughter. We were so in love and the ranch I'd inherited and reworked made us both happy." He shook his head, then rubbed a hand over his forehead, his heart racing with each memory. "He showed up wanting work a few months. I'd hired Rena to help Emma with the kids and I'd been looking for extra hands to help with everything around here. Rena lived close and drove over from a small town about eight miles from here. She had just become a widow. After her military husband went back for one more mission after a quick trip home, he got killed—an explosion."

"That's horrible." Lorelai lowered her head for a moment.

Drake lifted his chin. "Yeah, rough. We thought it would help her to be here with us as much as possible. Back then, we lived in the original smaller ranch home my parents built long ago." He stopped and cleared his throat. "We were almost finished with this place. My gift to Emma and the kids."

Lorelai registered that information, her expression softening as she heard the grief in his words. "Where are your children now? Are they safe?"

"They're both in college. We don't talk much and they don't know all the details of what happened."

Lorelai accepted that for now. "Go on."

"Emma asked me to give her half-brother a second chance. Her dad remarried after her mother died of cancer. Booker stayed in trouble and he and my father-in-law didn't get along. I gave him an opportunity to clean up his act—for Emma's sake and because I knew the wrath of her wealthy daddy." Drake shrugged. "He never liked me, either. She said her dad wasn't kind to Booker after he divorced Booker's mother. Treated him horribly and criticized him all the time."

Lorelai gazed at him, her expression now full of understanding and interest. "So you took Booker in and he messed up again?"

"He did." Drake sat up straight and cradled his hands against his blue jeans. "He got in a fight with one of my best workers, stole money from another man in the bunkhouse and would have stolen from me if I hadn't caught him."

Lorelai got up and moved toward the fire. "Go on."

He let go of a breath, then stared into the fire, the ache that never left him burning through his system. He refrained from telling her more. The marshal only needed the facts, not his family history. "We were here at the new house going over some things when I heard what he'd done. We had an argument and I fired him. He took off on foot, headed toward his old truck parked at the gate. And he had a gun—waved it at me a couple of times before he left. Emma got upset, ran out and took off on my horse—a big stallion we named Buster. I'd left Buster grazing near the new-build."

Lorelai stood still, then closed her eyes. "What happened next?"

Drake figured she'd already guessed. "Gunfire frightened Buster and he got mad as a hornet. Started bucking like a rodeo champ. Emma…she got thrown and hit her head on a big rock."

"Oh, no." Lorelai put a hand to her lips. "I'm so sorry, Drake."

"Yeah, me, too." Drake sank back, the telling of this taking its toll. "Booker saw Buster galloping through the trees and thought I was after him. He fired, knowing he would agitate Buster and possibly hit me. But it wasn't me. It wasn't me."

Lorelai sat down next to him. Bixby picked up on the tension and gave her a glance, his ears up. "So the shot caused Emma's death and you blame Booker and yourself?"

Drake nodded. "Things got ugly, and I wish I could have done something to stop him. I knew he'd retaliate eventually, but I never dreamed he'd do something so deliberate. I wanted to kill him, tried to get to him. He got in his truck and took off after I screamed at him." He stopped, dragged in a breath. "I couldn't leave Emma." Heaving for air, he looked at the woman beside him. "She was lying there so still, so beautiful. I saw the blood. I knew. I couldn't leave her."

Lorelai sat down beside him and put her hand over his, her

eyes burning with anger and sympathy. "I'll get him this time, Drake. I'll bring him to justice."

Drake lowered his head and wiped his eyes. "Well, I hope I'll be there to make sure you do that."

THREE

"You need to stay out of this," she replied. "You're too caught up in that day and what happened. We know he's wanted for murder so why do you think he came back all these years later?"

Drake turned and gave her a direct stare. "Because he shouted that he'd come back and kill me one day." Drake shrugged. "I shouted the same to him—that if he ever came back here, I'd kill *him*. But that wasn't true. I couldn't kill him, because of Emma. She steadied me, brought me back to the Lord and kept me from doing such deeds. I had to honor that." He rubbed his hands over his jeans. "Booker knows that, too, so he'll put me to the test."

Lorelai let that sink in. "Now that he's killed already and he's a wanted criminal, he's got nothing to lose. It took us months to find him and arrest him for the North Dakota murder, and now he's back on the run and could hide out on this place for a long time to come."

"Exactly. He's finally returned to finish me off. He blames me for Emma's death. He can get in line. I blame myself and him." Drake shook his head. "Who did he kill in North Dakota and when?"

"Richard Mitchell, earlier this year. A rancher. From what I've gathered, he led a quiet life and volunteered within the community, until according to the locals I interviewed, he lost everything and started drinking. He and Gleason got in a fight out behind a bar. Gleason fled but was caught after he committed another assault just over the state line." She shook her head. "Last week, he jumped one of the guards taking him to prison to wait for his trial."

"And he headed straight here." Drake's eyebrows went up and his jaw tensed. "That sounds like Booker. He had a bad temper and no self-control."

"I'm seeing that in him, yes."

Drake cleared his throat and threw up his hands. "Before Booker left way back, he got in a fist fight at a local bar. Messing with one of the waitresses, insulting her. Emma used to caution him about things like that, but Booker didn't care."

Drake's voice trailed off while he stared into the crackling fire. She had to keep asking questions he didn't want to answer, hear things he didn't want to tell her.

"Apparently Booker has some unfinished business with you."

"You can say that again."

"But to wait twenty years to come back here?"

"He's been running for a long time. I kept track of him for a while and then he went off the radar. I thought he'd died or left the country or got thrown in jail somewhere. He's a smart man who could never get his life together. I'm not surprised he escaped. He's gone off the deep end and he wants revenge. He wants to get even with everyone who turned him away." Drake tapped his boot on the floor. "Especially me."

"Makes sense," Lorelai replied. "We don't have proof that he's killed anyone else. I didn't find any aliases, but that doesn't mean he didn't take someone else's name illegally for a while. Happens all the time."

Drake's eyebrows shot up. "He knew exactly when to come. I always give my workers time off during the holidays. I only have two men here helping me right now."

"You're telling me we might not have backup?"

"I'm telling you this storm might knock out the power lines and we won't be able to reach anyone for help."

"You said you have two men here. Can we reach them?"

"I have a few who stay—no family to speak of. I'll alert them right now if I can find anyone in the bunkhouse."

They both looked at each other.

"The bunkhouse," he said, a frown narrowing his rugged face. "He'd head straight there."

Lorelai stood and checked her weapon. "We need to see if he did just that."

"Let me call one of my men first. The temperature will drop quickly now that dark is settling in and this storm will get worse. You don't want to go hunting during a whiteout."

Lorelai waited as he made the call, her mind racing with every possible scenario. Known to be impulsive, she obsessed about finding fugitives and bringing in criminals. Had she gone too far this time?

No, because Booker Gleason had come here with a definite intent to do harm and she had come here to stop him.

Drake could have been killed if she hadn't warned him. Or had she brought Booker right to him? Did Drake know more than he was saying?

Telling herself to stop second-guessing things, she whirled when she heard footsteps coming down the stairs.

A petite woman with a dark braid of hair tugged at her heavy robe and stared at Lorelai. "Are you staying the night?"

Lorelai glanced around, wondering how to answer that. Bixby's ears perked up. Whipping out her badge, she said, "I'm US Marshal Lorelai Danvers. I came here in search of a fugitive and Mr. Corbin and I were shot at while sitting in the kitchen. We went in pursuit, but the weather made it difficult to track the shooter."

The other woman went pale, her eyes widening in surprise before her gaze darted around the house. She came down the stairs and gave Lorelai a quick smile before glancing at Bixby's working vest. "What a nice partner you have there, Marshal Danvers. I'm Drake's sister, Rena Foster. I run this house."

"Oh, right. Drake mentioned you." Lorelai noticed icy blue

eyes and an oval face. Rena would be in her early fifties maybe. Her expression held no room for nonsense. Maybe there was more here than her being a housekeeper. An older sister watching out for her family legacy and her widowed brother? Could that be why she'd asked Lorelai about staying?

Rena searched the den. "I'm sure he did. I heard gunshots, but that's nothing new around here. Is he injured?"

"No, he's on the phone." Lorelai pointed toward the window where Drake paced back and forth.

"He doesn't look happy," Rena said, her furry booties hitting the steps down to where Lorelai stood.

Lorelai looked at the petite woman. "This snowstorm is not cooperating."

"They rarely do and this one seems to be a doozy," Rena said, studying Lorelai again. "What's your partner's name?"

"Bixby. He's a trained tracking dog."

"That makes sense," Rena said, smiling at Bixby. "A beautiful partner. Australian shepherds are a special breed."

"You're right there," Lorelai agreed. "Bixby is one of the best."

Bixby's ears lifted and he wagged his tongue with pride.

Drake turned around, his phone in his hand. "I can't get anyone to respond and I know Charles Hunter and Rex Salter were staying behind. They've both been with me for years so they tend to watch sports and let the younger workers go out on the town. They also volunteer to stay during the holidays. One of them should have responded."

"Let's go check it out," Lorelai said. "We can make it to the bunkhouse before the storm worsens, right?"

"I hope so," Drake said. "Grab your coat and put on your hat and gloves. You need to be covered from head to toe." He stopped and stared out the window. "We could take the ATV, but it tends to heat up in too much snow and it's loud. Or we can go on foot."

"On foot would be quieter if it's not too far and if we don't get lost."

"It's about a half mile and there's a trail."

"I need to get Bixby's snow boots," she replied. "I'll be right back."

Telling Bixby to stay, she checked the porch and hurried out to her SUV. After grabbing her backpack and other equipment, Lorelai turned to go back to the house. Looking down to watch her steps, she noticed something.

"What?"

One of the tires had been slashed and now lay flat and almost hidden in the deep snow. Then she smelled gasoline.

Holding a pen light under the SUV, she found a small hole in the gas tank. She wouldn't be going anywhere tonight, snow or no snow.

"Nice move, Gleason," she called out. He must have hurried back to the house after shooting at them in the woods. When she heard rustling in the bushes on the left side of the porch, she dropped the big pack and crouched behind her vehicle, waiting for the opportunity to confront Gleason at last.

"More where that came from," the man called back. "You can't stop me."

Lorelai crouched and slid around the SUV, her gun raised. "Gleason, don't do this."

Booker Gleason lifted up and took a shot at her. "I'm never stopping. You shouldn't have come here, Marshal."

He knew why she was here.

He must have been watching when she arrived, or maybe before. It made sense now. They couldn't track him because he knew this ranch and knew where to hide. Until now.

"Wrong, you shouldn't have returned here," she hurled back, rising to get in her own shot. Bixby growled low. Lorelai crouched and shot, covering herself until she could get around her vehicle. Glancing around, she listened as she hid near the back right fender.

Another shot echoed over the yard and then a boom.

The front of her SUV exploded like a bomb, knocking her

back into the snow. He'd hit the SUV's dripping gas tank. Lorelai saw some heavy shrubs and started toward them for cover and to get away from the fire. Before she could move, someone grabbed her from behind and slammed her against the SUV.

"You made a bad mistake tracking me here, Marshal. I ain't going back to jail and I'm sure not going to prison."

He tried to tug her closer to the flames.

Lorelai heaved a breath and stared into Booker Gleason's eyes. "You're wrong there," she said, fighting against him with one hand while she tried to aim her weapon. Then she shouted, "Bixby, attack."

The big dog leaped into the air and rushed toward Gleason before he could even think about shooting. The distraction gave her enough time to trip the man and kick him in the shin so she could get away from the burning vehicle. Gleason screamed and lunged at her, but Bixby stopped him, the dog's teeth tearing into his baggy pants. The fabric broke and Gleason jumped up and ran into the dark, shooting bullets from a handgun.

"Heel," Lorelai called to Bixby as she ran toward the house. "Come, Bixby."

The K-9 turned around and followed her until she moved away from the fire. Her SUV was toast.

"Good boy," she said. Trying to catch her breath, she listened. Gleason's footsteps were shielded by the snow.

She'd lost him again.

Another loud boom hit the air. "Come!" Lorelai shouted to Bixby as fire and shrapnel shot out all around them. She ducked and held Bixby behind her.

The front door burst open while another round of bullets exploded through the trees nearby. Lorelai shot back until she heard trees snapping.

"Stop," she called out, running toward the woods.

Drake hurried down the steps, rushing to her. "I heard the shots and saw someone," he said. "By the big windows." Then he watched as several remaining booms echoed around them. More hot metal sizzling against the cold snow.

Dragging her back, he held a hand up over his eyes. "He blew up your vehicle?"

"Yep. He attacked me and tried to push me into the explosion. Bixby got in some bites, but Gleason got away. Let me get to Bixby and get his boots on. He might be able to track Gleason."

Drake took off around the corner of the house, then hurried back to her. "It's useless," he told her after she picked up the big black canvas backpack and her other equipment. He urged her toward the house. "He's playing cat and mouse with us now."

"Well, I'm the cat and he's the mouse."

Drake looked her over. "Tell me again what happened out here?"

"He jumped me from behind. Bixby attacked him and tore his jeans. Might have gotten some flesh, too. Gleason ran away and I couldn't risk sending Bixby after him. Not in that snow."

"You need to be careful. He blew up your SUV and tried to kill you just now."

"He slashed one of my tires and put a hole in my gas tank. I can't leave, but I can go after him."

She left Drake standing by the windows and hurried inside to put on Bixby's heavy waterproof booties, making sure the Velcro fasteners would keep the dark thick canvas secure.

"Let's go," she called out to Drake. "Which way?"

Rena paced near the fireplace, her pretty face now edged with worry. "Who are you trying to track?" she asked Drake when he hurried in, a look of dread coloring her face.

Drake glanced at Lorelai before turning to Rena. "Booker Gleason."

Rena's eyes filled with shock and she put a hand to her heart. Lorelai didn't miss the look of sheer fear floating across the woman's face. Rena looked at Drake. "Booker is back?"

Drake nodded. "He's killed a man up north. He's probably

here to finally kill me. He tampered with the marshal's vehicle so it would leak gas and explode."

Rena gasped and lowered her gaze to the fire. "Booker knows this land and he knows how to hide." She pivoted, her gaze shifting from Drake to Lorelai. "Be aware. He'll set this whole place on fire if he can."

"I'm always aware," Lorelai replied, wishing she had time to take this conversation deeper. Something had passed between Rena and Drake, and she really wanted to know more about that something. Throwing on her coat and hat, she called, "Drake?"

Drake came up the hallway dressed for the weather, his rifle in his hand. "You need to listen to me and do as I say, Marshal Danvers. Understand?"

"I'm beginning to," Lorelai admitted. "I'll do what has to be done to stop Gleason."

"Me, too," Drake retorted.

"Me, three," Rena called. "I have my pistol ready. But what about that explosion?"

"The snow took care of that and we'll need to leave what's left for the crime scene techs," Lorelai replied.

"Set the alarm and lock up. Don't go all cowboy on me, Rena," Drake retorted. "You hear me? I've got enough to deal with here."

"You sure do," Rena replied with a brittle chuckle that seemed more apprehensive than humorous. The humor didn't reach the woman's eyes. "I know how this works, Drake."

Lorelai gave Rena a quiet appraisal, noting that touch of fear in her brave words. "Do as he says," she told Rena. "Don't let anyone in besides us."

"I don't think this is a laughing matter," Drake said to Lorelai in a whisper once they were walking to the back door. "I do agree about one thing."

"What's that?" Lorelai asked as they went through a big garage to get to the east side of the house.

"We need to take Booker Gleason out before he kills again."

* * *

"You can't shoot him without probable cause," Lorelai cautioned as they stomped through the deepening snow. "You realize that, right?"

Drake gave her a raised-eyebrow glance from underneath his Stetson. "I have probable cause. He's an intruder on my property and it will certainly be self-defense."

She wouldn't argue with him right now. Drake Corbin didn't want to take orders. That could make this mission much more dangerous.

"I can call in backup," she said when they stopped by some huge trees. "I know some of the task force team I'm with are available during the holidays. West Cole is a detective in Plains City, and part of the task force I served with earlier this year."

"I doubt anyone can get here right now," he said, glancing around the snow-covered forest beyond the wide-open fields. "This storm could turn into a whiteout, which means we'd get lost immediately and the temperatures alone can kill you. Calling for help might be a good idea once this storm is over."

"Where are we going?" she asked, thinking she'd have to really get familiar with how to survive in deep snow and below zero temperatures. At times like this, she sure missed Savannah and her beach hangout, Tybee Island.

"The bunkhouse is to the east of the main house. We can take the back trail until we see the security lights." He pointed to his left. "See that open spot between the thicket of trees. That's the trail."

"Okay, then let's get to it."

Bixby growled.

"I agree with your partner," Drake said. "Someone is on that trail."

"So how do we get there?"

"We stay in the woods on the edge of the tree line. We might find him before he finds us."

She nodded and shivered. "Bixby is good at picking up scents. He'll do what I tell him if things get rough."

"I'm guessing you expect me to do the same."

"That would make my job easier."

When they heard muffled noises up ahead, Drake tugged Lorelai behind some bramble. With a hand signal, she ordered Bixby to stay quiet.

The dog stood as still as stone. She tried to do the same. Drake's presence warmed her freezing bones, making her aware of him. She didn't need that kind of distraction tonight. *Focus. Focus.* Taking a breath, she studied the woods and the trail.

Drake guided her through the trees, snow falling all around them, their boots digging deep into the white mush. Lorelai had never been so cold in her life. The tension between them and her need to find Booker Gleason ran through her with a white-hot fire. She wanted this done and soon.

When they heard a moan, Drake stopped, holding her behind him as if he'd done that many times to protect someone else. That gesture rattled her professionally and touched her personally, making her feel warm and safe. Underneath all that gruff, Drake Corbin was a gentleman. And while that brought out feelings she'd long left dormant, right now she had to focus on finding the criminal who'd just tried to kill her.

Between the darkness and the reflections on the snow that gave them a bit of light, they followed the sound of the moans. Finally, they reached a curve where the trail became more secure.

Drake squinted into the dark mound on the snowy path. "There," he whispered. "Someone is hurt." He tugged Lorelai around. "You stay here and cover me. I think it's one of my men."

Lorelai nodded and got into position, Bixby now trembling to go beside her.

Drake took off through the trees and came crawling out of the woods near where the person lay. Then he leaned over and tugged the moaning figure close.

"Drake, go back," the hurt man shouted. "It's a trap. He's gonna kill you."

Drake didn't have time to react. His rifle lay out of reach in the snow, so he dove to the ground. Gunshots pounded, ricocheting off trees and heavy patches of ice and bramble, hitting around Drake and the other man.

Lorelai watched in horror. "Bixby, search." She took off through the trees, shooting as she went. The snow made everything look different. Even Bixby's salt-and-pepper coat seemed to blend with the snow and tree trunks.

Listening between cover shots, she decided the shooter might be up ahead and across the trail so she aimed her weapon to the west and fired several rounds. When she heard a hiss and a string of profanity, she knew she'd hit someone.

And she hoped that someone was Booker Gleason.

The shooting stopped, the silence as deadly as the gunfire she'd just heard. She ordered Bixby to halt while she tried to go to Drake and his worker.

Bixby stood barking into the woods as she approached Drake on the road, indicating activities nearby.

"Stay," she told Bixby again. The dog stood rigid, his gaze fastened on the trees.

She bent down beside Drake, her gaze going over the still body. "Who is this?"

"Charles Hunter," Drake said in a thick whisper. "Shot in the chest. He just died in my arms." He looked out into the cold night. "And I don't know where Rex Salter is."

Lorelai touched his heavy canvas barn jacket. "I'm sorry, Drake. I think I hit Booker."

"I hope you killed him," Drake said, his voice rusty with pain and regret. "I want him off my ranch for good this time."

FOUR

Lorelai knew Drake would make good on that promise. All the more reason for her to continue her duty. "What do you want to do, Drake? I need to track Gleason."

"Let's keep going," he said in a rush. "I can't do anything for Charlie right now. I'll move his body off the path. And I need to find Rex. He might be hurt or dead, too." He let out a huffy sigh. "Charlie was a good man. Lost his wife just like me. Came here broken and angry at the world."

"You helped him?" Lorelai could hear the pain shredding Drake's words as she helped him carry his friend across to the thicket near the path.

"We helped each other. I'd started drinking too much after Emma died. But we both got sober and clean...churchgoers, trying to do right, you know?"

"I do know," she replied. "I certainly understand."

"I'm sorry," he said. "Let's get this done. It's cold and Gleason is somewhere watching."

She motioned to where Bixby stood. "He's in there and he's stopped shooting. I need to verify if he's dead or alive."

The whole conversation and getting Charles moved had taken only seconds yet no one had shot at them. Had she killed Booker Gleason?

Bixby perked up when she gave him the Go signal. The dog moved through the snow and trees, his nose lowering down to the soggy ground and back up into the frigid air. When he took them to a spot that led back to the trail, Drake pointed toward a long rectangular building about a fourth of a mile away.

"The bunkhouse," he whispered. "I see a light burning."

Bixby headed that way.

"Someone is in there," Lorelai said. Then she pointed to the snow.

Drake shined a pen light down and saw it. Red spots leading to the front porch of the bunkhouse.

"I think we've found our man," he said, his voice gritty with anger. "Let's go."

Drake went first, his rifle out. Lorelai didn't fuss about him putting himself between her and danger. She stayed close to him and let Bixby take the lead, holding her own weapon up for protection.

They'd only gone a few feet when the air filled with white-hot heat and the bunkhouse exploded into a million pieces. Lorelai gasped as the heat and debris shot toward them, knocking them both to the ground. Drake fell across her, covering her with his upper body. Bixby went into a barking frenzy as he flew into the air and landed in the snow behind her.

Lorelai moaned and then her world went black.

Drake's ears rang with a burning chime, causing him to hold his hands against his head. Shaking it off, he saw his hat lying in the snow. Bixby rushed up to him, barking and whining.

"You okay, buddy?" Drake asked, still disoriented. Bixby danced around, then hurried a few feet away. The shaggy dog didn't exhibit any signs of being injured.

Lorelai.

Drake dragged himself out of the snow and ran to where Lorelai lay on an embankment, silent and still.

He sank down on his knees, the cold wet snow chilly as moisture saturated his jeans. Drake gulped in the cold air, his head lifted to the stormy sky.

"No," he said, calling out to the world. "Not again. Gleason, I won't allow you to hurt anyone else." Lorelai had come here to help him and now she was injured.

Falling down beside her, he checked her pulse. "Alive. That's good." He inhaled another deep breath to calm his wildly beating heart. Bixby stood close, his dark eyes on his human partner. "She'll be all right, boy. I hope."

Drake took another deep breath as he checked her for wounds. "Nothing broken." He finally lifted her head, afraid he'd feel sticky blood there. "No blood."

Lorelai moaned and tried to sit up. "Let's go."

"No, we can't." He held her down. "You're hurt. Your head."

She drifted back, her eyes closing. Clutching her right temple, she moaned again. "That hurts."

"I know," he replied, hearing the fierceness coursing through her whispers. "Just lay there for a minute. I need to call for help."

Drake sank back, watching the bunkhouse burn. Pulling out his phone, he tried to call 911. "No signal."

Touching Lorelai's head, he felt an inch-wide knot behind her right ear. "I have to get her home before this storm gets worse," he told Bixby.

The dog hovered, his demeanor quiet and protective, his furry body shivering with the need to take care of business.

Lorelai reached out a hand to her partner. "Bixby?"

The K-9 sniffed her with a gentle check. "Is Bixby okay?"

"He's fine," Drake said. She patted Bixby's head, then closed her eyes.

Drake tried his phone again to call Rena. He managed to get through. "Is everyone okay?" Rena asked. "I'm sitting on pins and needles here."

"I don't know yet. The bunkhouse is on fire and the storm's interfering with my phone. See if you can get a call to 911."

He wouldn't tell her about Charlie yet. She and Charlie were friends, but she and Rex had been dating for a while. He prayed

Rex was okay. Rena would be devastated if she lost Rex. She'd never liked Booker and had her own grief to bear.

"Drake? Drake?"

They lost contact. Deciding he needed to get the marshal back to the house, Drake shook his head and looked up at the snowflakes shimmering all around him.

This was turning into a bad one.

Once again, Booker Gleason had killed someone he loved. Charlie was gone.

And once again, he couldn't go after Gleason because he wouldn't leave Lorelai here alone in the snow. Instead, he took off his jacket and gently placed it around her to keep her warm. He found her gun and slung his rifle over his shoulder, then after he searched the area to make sure they were safe, he lifted her up in his arms.

She moaned and opened her eyes. "Drake?"

"Shhh. You're injured. This hunt is done for now."

"No."

"Yes."

She winced and laid her head against his shoulder. "I'm not happy about this."

"Neither am I."

Bixby hadn't bulged from his spot right next to her.

"Bixby?" she asked. "Come."

Drake knew better than to command the trained K-9. Lorelai had mentioned a name earlier. West Cole. A detective. He'd get in touch with the officer if the house phones were working. They needed help here.

He watched Bixby to see what would happen. The dog glanced at him, sniffed the air and after hearing Lorelai's whispered command, made a firm decision to follow him.

"Let's hope we make it to the house," Drake told Bixby. "I'll take care of her, Bixby, I promise."

The dog trotted behind him without a whimper or growl.

Drake kept glancing back along the trail, wondering if Gleason could be following them.

"Or maybe he's dead," he mumbled to himself. Now it was his turn to get revenge.

Once they had Lorelai on the big sofa by the fire, his sister took over. Used to taking care of business, she remained quiet and stoic. She'd check Lorelai over good and proper. Drake went into his office to use the house line to call the Plains City Police Department only to find the line dead.

The weather or Gleason?

Drake studied his surroundings. The bunkhouse was a lost cause even though the snow had stopped most of the flames. He wanted to find Gleason and he worried about Rex.

His reclusive ranch had just become a murder scene.

Drake didn't know Lorelai Danvers very well, but he knew enough to see she would be relentless in finding an at-large criminal. He figured something drove her desire to bring justice to the world. Who had hurt her?

He prayed and whispered, "I will find him, Lorelai. We'll find him. You have to wake up."

Maybe another day, they could talk to each other like normal people over a good steak dinner. A nice-looking, smart woman had risked her life to warn him about Booker Gleason. He owed her a good dinner, at least.

"You need to wake up and start arguing with me."

What if she didn't? He'd only known her a couple of hours, yet it seemed like a lifetime. Her showing up at his door had triggered all the horrible memories he'd tried to shut down. She'd also triggered something in his hard heart.

She believed in justice and so did he. Only he'd made a promise to Emma that he wouldn't use violence to solve his problems. He'd kept that promise for many years because he'd believed Gleason would never show his face at this ranch again.

Gleason aimed to take Drake out before he went down. He'd

also take anyone else out so Drake had to protect his family and Lorelai.

Rena called into his office. "Drake, she's awake."

Drake hurried into the den and found Lorelai frowning.

"What happened?" Lorelai asked, her eyes wide with a let's-go glare. She tried to sit up. "We were on the trail."

"Yes, and the bunkhouse exploded." He glanced back at the kitchen, then lowered his voice. "Charlie Hunter is dead."

Lorelai bounced up, her hand going to her head. "I remember. We were after Gleason and I shot at him, might have injured him. I need to go back."

"Not just yet," Drake said, urging her down. "You have a knock the size of an egg on your head."

"I'd been knocked out before," she protested, looking toward the floor where her wet boots sat, Bixby laying nearby. "We almost had him. He might be dead."

"Then he'll lay there until we get someone out here to help us," Drake replied. "Right now, the house phone is not working and my cell is in and out. If he's injured, he won't get far."

"He's been hiding here, Drake. Probably for days. Now he's killed again and caused two explosions on your property. Doesn't that bother you just a bit?"

"You know by now it bothers me a lot," he retorted, his frustration making heat rise up his neck. "I have people coming and going. They've all been vetted and approved. One of them could have helped harbor a fugitive. If I find out that, they will pay dearly."

Rena came back and stood by the wide door to the kitchen. "I can't believe Booker is out there."

Drake shot Rena a shuttered glance. "I'll find him."

Lorelai tried to sit up again, her eyes burning fire. "First we have to get to him."

Drake tugged her back down. "Marshal, I admire your determination, but we are not going back out there. The storm is getting worse. I tried to reach your friend at the police department and the call kept dropping."

"You called West?"

"He's the only name you mentioned. Thought I'd start there. I'll try again when this blizzard calms down." He stared at Lorelai, his gaze unyielding. "And once you're better."

She settled back on the couch. "I'm fine. Just a nagging pain." Running a hand over her mushed hair, she winced. "I think a piece of shrapnel hit me."

"You must have a hard head. I didn't find any blood."

She frowned at Drake, her head pounding in protest. "I *must* be an idiot to come out here on a night like this. Knowing he's here only makes things worse."

"You did your duty, Marshal. Now do me a favor and sit there and behave yourself. Let's see if we can reach your friend for backup."

Lorelai glared at him, then fell back against the pillow. Rena came in with an icepack and some hot tea. "You'll live, but you need to stay awake a while. I'll give you some pain pills after you eat a bite or two."

"I'm not hungry."

"Then drink this herbal tea."

"Did you know Booker, too?" Lorelai asked Rena.

Rena's gaze widened. "We all knew him."

That didn't really answer Lorelai's question. Drake's own instincts starting tickling against his skin. Rena was acting strange, but then this was all strange and aggravating.

"Drink," Rena coaxed. "Focus on yourself for now."

Lorelai's frown grew while she sipped the tea.

Rena believed in holistic medicine so no telling what was in that herbal tea, but it should calm Lorelai's aching head. His sister had had a visceral reaction to hearing Gleason had come back. Drake was worried about her. She'd never liked Booker Gleason or the way he treated women.

He had his own reaction to deal with. This whole situation had only reminded him of Emma's horrible death. He should have killed Booker Gleason long ago. Only Emma's faith in God and in Drake had kept him from doing so.

Now he had another woman in his life. One who'd shown up and set this night into motion. And with the snow thickening and no end in sight, he had a feeling she'd be here for a few days, at least. And he also had a feeling she wasn't going to give up until she carted Booker Gleason away in a police van.

Lorelai finished her tea, then glanced up at Drake. "I'm sorry about your friend Charlie."

On her way back from the kitchen, Rena whirled toward Drake. "What happened to Charlie?"

Lorelai glanced at Drake and he turned to face Rena. "I'm sorry, Rena. He didn't make it."

Rena went white in the face, then sank down onto the ottoman across from the sofa, her hand to her lips. "And Rex?"

"We didn't see him," Drake said, a hand touching his sister's arm. "But you know how tough Rex is. He'll let me know something soon, I'm sure."

Rena abruptly stood and turned to Drake and Lorelai. "Find him, no matter what it takes. Find that killer."

Drake dropped his hands to his sides. "We aim to do just that. I know how close you are to Charlie and Rex."

Rena held her head up. "You're right. We're all close, but Rex and I..." She stopped, her back to them. "Booker being back here. This is about so much more, Drake."

Drake nodded. He could feel Lorelai's gaze burning through him.

"We're going to get him off this land," he said to Rena. "You know I'll do it."

"I'm here to help with that," Lorelai reminded both of them.

Drake only hoped he could live up to bringing Gleason to justice. From the look in Lorelai's eyes, she seemed to be thinking the exact same thing.

FIVE

Two hours later, without a vehicle and with a snowstorm raging, Lorelai sat on the sofa with her cell phone, trying to pull up her notes on Booker Gleason while Drake did a quick surveillance walk outside. Iffy reception and messy weather didn't help. Rena had explained how whiteouts worked. Visibility limited to inches, disorientation taking over, getting lost and confused. Cold howling wind that brought the wind chill well beyond normal chilly temperatures. Freezing to death in a matter of minutes.

Would Gleason survive out there?

Annoyed that she was stuck here with a hurt head until the storm ended, she planned to use this time to corner Drake regarding what Rena had said earlier about this being so much more.

She had a feeling he held his torment close to his heart, hiding away from the world as much as possible. For a place this huge, he had very little security and a small working staff. He also had the tough skin of a man who made his own rules.

That could be good or bad.

Rena came back into the den. "I have your room ready, Lorelai. I'll wash what you're wearing. I have some of my son's clothes here. Things he outgrew that I kept. They're clean."

"You have a son?" Lorelai liked Rena and saw her strong loyalty to Drake. She needed to dig deeper with the dedicated housekeeper. Lorelai's instincts told her Drake and his sister had more than just grief between them. Too many worried glances and cryptic remarks. Too many dark expressions on their faces. Too many questions in her throbbing head. "Does your son live here, too?"

"He died three years ago," Rena replied in a stoic tone, her blue eyes misty. "A bad crash up on the highway. Got hit by a drunk driver who left the scene. He had just turned sixteen."

Lorelai stood and ignored the dizziness making her see two of the older woman. "I'm so sorry, Rena."

"This place is drenched in grief," Rena said as she gazed around the minimalist-style house. "Drake keeps it as a shrine to Emma and I have nowhere else to go. But I also love it despite the sadness that moves through these walls. It's where my son grew up with his cousins."

Surprised, Lorelai took a long look at the rustic mansion while she refrained from asking more questions. She'd let Rena talk. "It's all glass and stone."

"And yet dark at times," Rena replied. "Emma died before they finished building this house. They lived in a modest ranch house about a half-mile from here. The ranch foreman and his wife stay there now. They went out of town on a ski trip."

Lorelai took in that information, thinking Gleason might be hiding out in the empty house. She focused on Rena again. "Drake told me you were widowed at a young age, but he didn't mention your son. It must have been difficult raising a child without your husband."

"Yes," Rena replied, her shoulders squared, her eyes glazed with a faraway memory. "I worked here off and on as a babysitter while my husband was deployed. Right after Drake lost Emma…I realized I was pregnant. He gave me a full-time job and a place to stay. He needed someone to help with the kids, and I sure needed a lot of support back then. He was in a bad way. I guess we both were. We're family, after all."

"Booker came here too during that time, right?"

"Yes." Rena glanced out a window. "I've said too much. Let's get you to your room."

Rena had said too much? Something about his sister's reaction to Booker being back shouted at Lorelai right along with a detail she'd tried to pull up after the bunkhouse exploded, but between her aching head and all the questions gathering like a landslide in her mind, the thought left her.

Bixby alerted when they heard a door opening.

Drake entered the open hallway between the kitchen and the den, all bundled up and holding his rifle. "I thought you'd be in bed by now," he said to Lorelai, his frown ruthless and slightly agitated.

"And I thought you'd gone too far beyond the yard," she replied, glancing at the snow on his boots and back up to his face. "Find anything?"

Drake kept frowning then glanced at his sister. "Nothing much. The storm is getting worse." Then he took off his coat and threw it on the ottoman.

Rena took in a breath as she lifted the heavy coat and dusted it off, then started toward the stairs. "I'm going to bed. I left some clothes and toiletries upstairs. You can show Lorelai to her room."

"Good night." Drake stood, still frowning.

"Thank you, Rena." Lorelai paced, convinced they both knew something she didn't.

Bixby stood, his ears up, his head moving from one human to the other.

After Rena left, her footsteps echoing up the stairs, Drake put down the rifle and went to the fire. "I checked my property, but I don't need to answer to you, Marshal."

"No, and you don't need to get defensive with me, either. You and your sister are on edge and I understand that, but I need all the facts before this gets any worse."

"You're angry."

"I'm not. I'm eager. Eager to get the man who has now killed two people that we're aware of. The man who's gunning for you, and me, too, now that he knows I'm here with you."

"I didn't ask you to come. In fact, I didn't want to invite you into my home."

Lorelai decided the honeymoon was over. "Now you regret having to tell me the truth."

"What I regret, Marshal, is that I didn't take care of this all those years ago."

She understood now. "You're remembering. I'm sorry. Truly."

"I am remembering, and I'm also trying to protect my property, myself, Rena and you. I have that right."

"Okay, I can't blame you for going back out there. What did you find?"

He let out a breath, his features softening into a firm blankness. "I found footprints off the trail. I watched the last embers of the bunkhouse fade into the wet snow. And I searched for Rex. I couldn't find any blood or anything else because the snow is almost a foot deep now."

"Where would an injured man running from the law go in this kind of weather?"

"Into the woods, or wherever he could find shelter, warmth, food. Or he might wait it out under a tree."

"What about a house? Your foreman isn't home right now, according to Rena."

"Have you been nagging her?"

"I wasn't nagging. We were having a conversation about her life here. She offered me some of her son's clothes."

Drake's expression went back to dark. "She doesn't talk about Gerard."

And neither had he, Lorelai wanted to remind him. "She did tonight."

Drake sat down, his face traced with weariness. "We'll check the house first thing tomorrow. It's a whiteout right now."

Lorelai decided not to push him anymore with her questions and she couldn't try to do this on her own with the visibility so bad and her head still woozy. "I can't argue with that but in the meantime, I'll keep trying to reach West. This calls for a lot of reinforcements."

"I agree. If Gleason is still alive, and I'm beginning to doubt that, we will find him."

Lorelai nodded and headed toward the stairs. "Which way?"

"To the left," he said softly. "First room on the right."

She lifted her hand, whirled toward the stairs and promptly got dizzy.

Drake rushed to catch her but she held to the stair railing and blinked up at him. His eyes were so dark she thought she could be staring into an abyss. Dark and full of secrets.

"I can walk," she mumbled, her head still spinning, her throat raw with awareness, his outdoor scent making her even more dizzy.

He guided her into the room and then helped her sit down on the bed, his gaze glowing with a heat that made her look away. Drake moved closer, forcing her to look at him. "Try to rest."

"I'm fine." She kept her gaze on him, telling herself he wouldn't intimidate her. "I think I can sleep now without going into a coma."

"Okay, sleeping beauty. Tomorrow, we regroup."

"Drake?"

He turned just inside the doorway.

"Is there something, some secret, between you and Rena?"

His chuckle was brittle. "Nothing that I know of, but we are both private people. After what we've been through, Rena and I are as close as a brother and sister can be, yet we rarely talk. She takes care of this house and I take care of the land. We both watch out for my children." Drake stopped and glanced around the room. "Grief brought us close and grief keeps us quiet. We're not hiding much more than that."

"Not even about Booker?"

"What do you mean?"

"Your sister won't talk much about him."

"All I know is Rena never liked Booker. He was hard to like."

When she didn't respond, he held up a hand. "I'm telling you the truth, Marshal. If there was something brewing between them, she never told me."

"Thank you."

"For what?"

"For being honest about everything."

"Don't thank me yet. You might be here for a while."

"So I might drag more facts out of you."

"You never give up, do you, Marshal?"

"Part of my job, I'm afraid."

"Turn off that brain for now, okay."

After he shut the door, Lorelai looked at Bixby.

"I reckon he's correct on that, Bixby boy. I can't stop these thoughts racing through my head because I'm pretty sure he's *not* being completely honest with me."

The dog whimpered and sank down on the lush carpet.

Lorelai stared into the darkness, a shiver running down her spine. This was only the beginning.

An hour later, she woke in a sweat, a banging noise bringing her to her feet and causing Bixby to alert and growl low. Grabbing the robe Rena had provided, she tied it tight against the big sweatshirt she'd found in the closet with some other clothes, grabbed her firearm and signaled to Bixby before she headed downstairs, her throbbing head trying to catch up.

Drake met her on the stairs. "I got it," he whispered, pushing past her with a pistol. The man surely had weapons all over the house. Normal for a remote ranch in the badlands of South Dakota, she thought, as she raced down the stairs after him. Bixby followed, staying quiet after she commanded him with a signal.

Drake stood by a side door and motioned for her to stay behind him. Lorelai moved quietly toward him, then leaned against the wall. They both listened to the scraping sound coming from behind the door.

"That's the door near the garage," he whispered. "Only three or four people have the code."

"You and Rena and your two trusted older employees?" she asked in her own whisper.

"Yep, unless someone forced it out of one of them."

"Let's find out."

He nodded and turned to open the door, while she stood with her firearm aimed at the garage. "Don't shoot," he told her. "It might be Rex."

Drake took a breath, drew his pistol and slowly opened the big door. Lorelai watched as a man fell into the room, snow dropping off his coat and boots.

"Rex," Drake said, waving her away. "It's Rex Salter."

Lorelai let out a sigh full of frustration and relief. Glad Rex had survived, she had to wonder about Gleason. And if he was still alive.

Rena came running. "Rex!" She held her hand to her heart. "You're alive."

"Almost," the man quipped. "Good to see your pretty face."

Rena touched his arm and gave him a peck on the cheek, appearing too overcome to speak.

"Rex, are you injured?" Drake asked as he dragged the man inside and shut and locked the door. "Where have you been?"

"I'll live," his friend mumbled. "My feet probably have frostbite. I hid out where I could find warmth. I'm freezing."

Drake handed Lorelai his weapon and lifted his friend up to help him to the same couch she'd been on earlier. Lorelai placed both weapons on a console and grabbed pillows and blankets.

"Where have you been?" Drake asked. "Did you and Charlie split up?"

"We heard an explosion and figured it was a transformer. We'd put on jackets to go outside and check. When we opened the door, Booker Gleason stood there with a gun, threatening to kill us. Charlie ran one way and me the other. Gleason screamed something about blowing up the bunkhouse and that's what he did. We didn't have time to grab guns. Just ran out. I think he shot toward Charlie first after Charlie tried to disarm him, then he turned toward me. I ducked and hid out until I could figure out how to get here. Heard the explosion and saw the bunkhouse burning. Where's Charlie?"

Lorelai watched as the frazzled, world-weary man glanced around, his silver beard holding beads of ice. Then he looked back up at Drake. "Did he make it here yet?"

Drake sat down on the big ottoman. "I'm so sorry, but Charlie didn't make it, Rex. He's out there in the snow. I'm going to get him come daylight."

Rex said something underneath his breath, then huffed and cleared his throat. "Charlie's dead? I should have done more to stop this. What does Booker want, Drake?"

"Me," Drake said. "Gleason's come back to finish me off. And he'll kill everyone here to get to me."

Rex looked around at Lorelai. "And who is she?"

Drake's gaze danced over her. "This is US Marshal Lorelai Danvers. She's here for Gleason and now, well, she's stuck until this storm ends. He blew up her vehicle and tried to kill her."

Rex, a slender man who looked like he didn't trust anyone, gave her a long stare, his battered face forcing a tight smile. "Well, I'll be. You sure will come in handy around here."

"I hope so," Lorelai replied. "Right now, let's check you for wounds."

"Whoa," Rex said, waving her away. "Drake can do that."

"I'll get you something warm to drink," Rena said. "What would you like?"

"Bourbon," Rex replied without a beat. "But I'll settle for coffee."

"On the way."

Lorelai headed to the kitchen to help Rena.

"We rarely get any sleep around here and this night has been one of the worst," Rena said.

"It might get even worse before it's over," Lorelai replied. "We'll do what needs to be done."

Rena didn't respond. She just gave Lorelai a knowing nod, then started pulling out food for a sunrise breakfast. "Rex'll be hungry," she finally said. "Men are always hungry."

Lorelai had to agree with that. "I'm glad Rex is okay."

"So am I," Rena said, her gaze shifting to the shattered window Gleason had shot out earlier. "Booker shouldn't have come back here."

While Drake took care of Rex and asked him more questions, the two women worked in silence. Lorelai didn't miss the worry she saw in Rena's blue eyes nor the way Rena glanced toward Drake now and then. This woman who seemed to hold her own couldn't hide her fear of Booker Gleason. Understandable, considering all the harm he'd done, but Lorelai's gut told her there was even more history here.

Lorelai needed to find out for sure—and fast.

SIX

Rex explained again how shocked he was to see Booker standing at the bunkhouse door.

"He looked bad, Drake. Like he'd been living in the woods or something. Skinny and dirty and dangerous." Rex took a sip of coffee and nibbled at his toast and eggs. "He was loaded for bear, though. Didn't waste any time explaining why."

Lorelai had found a pen and paper in the kitchen to take notes. "What happened next?"

"He turned away and Charlie grabbed him and tried to stop him, but he knocked Charlie to the floor then started shooting. We dived down but couldn't get to our guns. After we split up, I heard gunshots and saw Charlie fighting with him again. Charlie stumbled. I went to help him, but Gleason started shooting again. Charlie told me to run. I tried to figure out a way to get to Gleason, but after all the gunfire he disappeared into the woods. I had to hide, too, so I ran the other way." He stopped and put down his fork. "I shoulda gone after Charlie. Shoulda searched for him out there."

"You would be dead now, if you'd done that," Rena said, her voice thick with pain. "I'm glad you're okay, Rex."

"Me, too. I can't believe Charlie's gone."

"Me, either," Drake replied, glancing at Rena. "He was one of the best."

Lorelai took it all in, seeing the loyalty between Drake and his staff. Would they hide the truth for him? Drake had told her the worst of it, yet her instincts signaled they were all covering something else. Her tired bruised brain wouldn't bring up the thoughts she needed to piece this together, so she could be imagining things.

"So you stayed in the woods for a while?"

Rex nodded at her. "I hurried to an old trail behind the bunkhouse, then did a turn toward the main house. Heard more shooting. With no phone, and just the clothes I'm wearing, I huddled under a tree, then made it to the stables and warmed up a bit before I came here. I wanted to get to Drake, tell him what happened. Found a horse blanket from the tack room and followed the security lights until I got to the garage and used the code. Almost passed out when I finally made it. Just sore from running and ducking, I reckon. I ain't used to sprinting in deep snow so I went flat-faced a couple of times."

Rena handed him fresh socks. "Your feet are okay. Still, you might need to get checked over. You boots are dry now. I set them by the fire."

Rex put on the warm socks and nodded. "That feels good. I guess I'll bunk here for the night."

"Yes, you will," Drake replied. "Take the downstairs bedroom. I'll stay here in the den and guard things."

"This ain't gonna end good, is it?" Rex asked, eyeing Drake.

"No, but between all of us, it will end one way or another."

Lorelai lifted her shoulders. "I'm not leaving here without Booker Gleason, dead or alive." She shrugged. "I don't even have a way to leave now."

"I like her," Rex said to the room in general.

Drake gave Lorelai a look traced with questions and a bit of awe. "She grows on you, that's for sure."

Drake didn't get much sleep. The couch faced the fire and he had lots of blankets. The storm howled with a vengeance that matched Drake's own. He could hear trees snapping in the wind while his mind kept spinning back to the past and the one opportunity he'd had to stop Booker Gleason. He'd watched the man, tracking him here and there through the years, but Booker wasn't as dumb as he acted. He'd managed to go to ground for years. Why he'd decide to return here now, during the thick of winter and with the law after him, Drake couldn't fathom. No one knew what went through Booker's mind. This blizzard had whitewashed the whole area. Roads were closed and everything had come to a halt.

Everything except the man who might still be out there, dead. Or very much alive and just waiting for his next strike.

"He's always had problems," Emma used to say. "Not good with socializing and has a mean temper. He can't control his rage. He and Daddy just never got along, and…I'm all he has, Drake."

Drake didn't mind giving people a second chance. But he did mind people who didn't appreciate anything, people who expected the world to do their bidding. Booker took what he wanted without considering the consequences.

He prayed they'd get this over with and soon. Lorelai was a distraction he didn't want or need. But she sure made a good distraction in a bad situation. He wondered how things could be if they'd met under better circumstances. Was he ready for anything like that?

Nope. No. Not gonna happen.

Rena came downstairs dressed for the day. "Did you get any sleep?"

"Not really." He stood and finished off the strong cup of coffee he'd made earlier. "I'm going out soon to check on the livestock and see what damage the storm did."

"The wind's settled but the snow is high, Drake. Why don't you stay in today?"

"I have to do what I can."

"And what about Booker?" she asked, barely whispering his name. "You could put yourself in more danger."

"Are you scared?"

Drake knew she'd never liked Booker when she'd come here as a young widow to help Emma. They'd buried her husband, Danny, a few weeks before she moved in with them. About a month in, she told Drake she was pregnant. A widow and pregnant. Danny had never known his son here on earth. They were both in Heaven together now. Rena shied away from dating and barely tolerated being around strangers. She never wavered on raising her son, however. Gerard grew up with Drake's kids, Susan and Clay. The day she'd lost Gerard had been just as horrible as the day she'd lost her husband and when he'd lost Emma.

"I'm worried," she said now, her face devoid of makeup and looking pale and frazzled. "I thought we'd never see him here again…after…"

"After what he did. After he caused Emma's death?"

She nodded. "I'll get breakfast going."

Drake stared at his sister, then looked up to see Lorelai coming down the stairs, Bixby behind her. "I've never seen Rena like this," he said, whispering low. "This has upset her. Maybe I'm missing something here, too."

Lorelai wore old jeans and a big sweatshirt, and her hair shimmered in ruffled dishevel around her face. "That's obvious. Did they spend time around each other?"

"Nope. She avoided him and he barely noticed her. After he left and Gerard was born, she kept up with her baby and our kids. She and Emma were really close."

The marshal wouldn't forget his words. He could see by the way she twisted her lips she'd started percolating theories inside that smart head. Had he missed something back then when he'd been so absorbed in his own grief?

"Coffee?" he asked, sending her toward the kitchen. "Rena is making breakfast. I'm on my way to check on Rex."

He used the excuse to stop her from questioning him more about Rena's past. Drake respected his sister's privacy and didn't nag his other workers about their personal lives. He only expected them to keep the peace and do their jobs.

Rena kept things together and they both honored each other's secrets. He wouldn't have made it without his older sister's help.

Lorelai took the hint and headed toward the kitchen to find the dog food she'd had in her go-bag. "Okay, I need to feed Bixby."

The bedroom door across the hall from the kitchen opened before Drake could knock.

"Morning," Rex said, still limping from where he'd fallen and hit a limb in his sprint last night. "I'm fine, Drake. No need to look so glum."

Drake nodded and followed his friend up the long hallway. "I know but I'm glum because we lost Charlie and Booker Gleason is back on my land. Not to mention I have a US marshal bunking in my house until the snow melts."

"Well, look at the bright side," Rex replied between bouts of coughing. "She's a pretty US marshal."

Drake couldn't argue with that. "Better than some who've shown up at my door."

His friend chuckled. "We gonna head out to the foreman's house?"

"Yep. Thought we'd take one of the off-road vehicles. We'll need to check on the livestock and make sure the windbreaks and stables are secure."

Lorelai plated their ham biscuits and scrambled eggs while Rena finished up at the stove. She motioned to the large island. "Have a seat, gentlemen. We've got a busy day ahead of us."

"I reckon that knot on your head must be better," Drake said. He grabbed a hot biscuit from the bowl she'd placed on the island. Bixby inhaled his dog food and drank up the water she'd placed by his food bowl.

After checking on her partner, she gave Bixby a signal and the dog dropped to the floor. "A bit sore. I've been through worse."

He wondered what all she had been through. He could ask questions when he wanted answers, too. And he had a lot of questions for this woman.

But not right now.

Lorelai had the look of a warrior on her face. Her eyes held that daze of awareness he'd seen in men before a long cattle roundup or a mission to find poachers and bring them to justice. The look of someone who wouldn't stop until they had what they'd come after. Most of the women he'd known had been strong in their own ways.

Lorelai Danvers was tough-strong. She wouldn't take any foolishness from anyone. Including him.

She glanced up from buttering her biscuit, her gaze chasing his. "We have a lot going on today, Drake. We need to get some backup here and you need to call the local coroner to take your friend's body to the morgue. First, we check the foreman house and then we search for Gleason as much as possible all across your property. Whatever happens, I'm in it for the long run. I want Gleason off the streets."

From the stove, Rena lifted her coffee mug. "I think we can all toast to that." Then she stepped toward the island. "I'll call the coroner—if I can get through."

Rex glanced from Drake to Lorelai. "I guess we just got our marching orders."

They finished eating fast and in silence and then headed to the end of the long garage. Drake and Rex had rifles and Lorelai had her handgun with two extra rounds of ammo. Drake noticed she'd put on her official black United States Marshal vest and had a backpack of essentials to help her. Bixby had a matching black vest that announced him as a working law enforcement K-9.

She'd grabbed her stuff before the SUV exploded. The thought of how close she'd come to being blown up made him sick to his stomach. Dangerous, yet this woman knew how to take care of business. She'd fought off a killer while the world exploded around her.

Drake could only pray that he'd be able to save her if she went all rogue on him. Which she'd probably do at some point in this hunt. The woman was scary-determined. And he had to admit, he felt the same way.

SEVEN

Lorelai and Bixby got on the ATV four-seater Drake cranked and drove out of the garage. She wondered whatever happened to cowboys on horses. The sleek black ATV had a snowplow and blower attached to the front, creating a path for them in the deep white snow covering the whole area.

Glad they had a canvas cover overhead, she glanced at him. "Impressive."

"It helps us clear paths, so we can get around faster to check on our livestock. And yes, we still have horses," he said, nodding as if he could see her thoughts. "They're safe and warm in the stables. I'll check on them after we clear the foreman house. Gleason wouldn't dare go to that house if he's got any sense left. He has to know we'd look for him there."

"He dared to come on your ranch," she replied in a firm rebuttal.

"Touché."

Rex followed them on a snowmobile, snow flying out in crystals behind him.

The cold took her breath away, but Lorelai didn't complain. She lifted her scarf to her nose, thinking she could handle the frigid air. Focusing on what might come, she took in the stark flat land and snow-covered limestone hills beyond the trees and pastures. The harsh rock face in the distance reminded her of

Badlands National Park a few miles from here. Had Gleason been hiding there, too?

"Won't he hear us coming?" she asked Drake over the motor's low roar.

"If he is in the house, he's probably doctoring his wound."

"If he made it this far."

"He's tough and he knows how these storms work."

She took that to mean Drake believed Booker could still be alive. Her gut told her the same.

"Where are your livestock?"

"We have bison and cattle," he replied, glancing here and there. "The bison can handle winter so they stay in the far pasture. Can't mix them with cattle. We move the cattle into pastures near here—the winter range—and have windbreaks for them to huddle together. Some are tree breaks and some are metal three-sized structures. We give them extra feed during the winter for this very reason. Keeps their metabolism going and that brings warmth. We have to make sure we feed them properly so they don't get sick. We can find water by chopping holes in the ice along the streams' beds."

"That's a lot of work. I can see it's necessary as a rancher in this brutal place."

He shot her a quick glance from underneath his tan suede cowboy hat. "It's also beautiful."

"I'm learning that, too."

She gave him a thumbs-up and stopped asking questions as they approached an open field with a small brown-paneled ranch house near a stand of trees off to the left.

Drake killed the engine and turned to her. "We continue on foot from here. You know the drill so be careful. Don't get lost in the snow, Marshal."

"Bixby and I are ready," she said, glancing back at the alert dog. "You should be careful, too, Drake."

Drake stared at the house. "I don't like coming back here.

Too many memories. He's hiding out in this house just to mess with my head."

"Don't let him do that," she replied, her tone soft but solid. "Stay focused on what matters right now."

"You're right. I can't go back. I can move forward in helping you capture him."

"Now you're talking my language."

"What is your language, Marshal?"

Lorelai didn't hold back. "My father was in law enforcement, and it left him bitter and angry. I don't want to be that person. My goal is to stay focused and seek justice, to make amends for what my dad went through."

"You have a need to please?"

"I have a need to put away criminals and keep people safe."

"Right." He saw through her. "What's the real story, Marshal?"

She shot him a side-eye then heaved a deep breath. "I tried to please my father but he hated that I chose the US Marshal program instead of the local good ole boys. He handpicked the man he wanted me to marry and while we did love each other, after a year or so we both agreed it wasn't working. Dad blamed me. So here I am about as far away from my home as possible. We all have our secrets, Drake."

Drake studied her, his dark eyes showing his torment. "I guess we do. I'm sorry you went through that." Then he looked away as the house came into view. His eyes met hers again. "Let's move in."

Lorelai's heart did a few extra beats. Not because of what they were about to do. She'd raided houses before and she'd found suspects and criminals hiding in strange places.

Drake had looked at her with a silent plea that begged her to stay clear of him and his pent-up grief and anger. He'd become a recluse for a reason, just like she'd left Georgia for a reason. He had never gotten over losing the love of his life, and she'd decided not to fall in love until it was on her own terms. Being near him had her heart doing weird little beats.

She should heed that subtle warning yet telling her heart that didn't make it any easier to do so. Reminding herself of her words to him, she focused on the task at hand. She certainly wasn't ready to go into another relationship, so why was she experiencing all these feelings she'd never had with anyone else each time she looked into Drake's eyes?

Maybe nerves and adrenaline. She'd use that to get this done and over. If and when this ended, she would be on her way and this ranch and Drake Corbin would be a memory to her. He'd forget her but he'd never forget this criminal who'd come back to taunt him.

She needed to finish the job, for Drake's sake. And for her own need to find justice. She motioned to Bixby and then Drake. She'd take the front and he'd circle to the back while Rex provided cover if needed.

"Let's go," she whispered, her mind thinking ahead to what they might find in that house. When they heard a door slamming shut, they each got in place behind trees and waited to see who would come running.

Nothing.

Lorelai glanced at where Drake sat crouched behind snow-covered trees. Had they heard wrong?

Rex stayed back, waiting with his rifle aimed at the front door. He shrugged.

"What's going on, Bixby?" she whispered to the dog. "Can you pick up his scent?" She'd allowed Bixby to sniff the puffer jacket she'd been wearing when Gleason had attacked her earlier.

She motioned to Drake to stay, then she signaled to Bixby to search. The fluffy K-9 galloped up to the house and sniffed around the door, then he moved to a row of windows on the right side of the house, lifting his nose in the air and back to ground.

Bixby zeroed in on a window to the right of the front door. Then he put his front paws down and turned back to Lorelai.

"Someone's in that room," she mouthed to Drake, her hand behind her to tell Rex to wait. "Let's go."

Drake nodded and slipped to the other side of the house.

Lorelai crouched behind bushes and trees until she had a direct line to the window where Bixby sat guarding. Her partner liked nothing better than tracing a scent to a suspect or criminal. With his loud bark and sixty-pounds of weight, Bixby could scare a suspect into surrendering in a matter of seconds. His bark was worse than his bite, but she never revealed that.

Thinking the best pursuit right now would be obvious, she hurried through the snow and knocked on the front door.

Bixby waited for whatever happened next. When she heard movement in the house, Bixby growled low and eyed the window above him. Sure enough, the window opened and a gun barrel extended out.

"Come on out," Lorelai said as she pressed against the wall of windows across from the door. "You're trespassing."

A gunshot shattered the bark off a tree about a foot away from where Rex crouched. Lorelai held up her hand to warn Rex, then moved toward the front door. Drake came around the back corner.

"A small snowmobile parked in the back," he whispered. "Stolen from the barn by the bunkhouse."

"Has to be him," she whispered back. Drake nodded and pointed before he moved to that side of the house. Lorelai leaned out toward the open window. "You need to come on out. It's over, Gleason."

Another round of shots. "It is not over until I've done what I came to do here, Marshal Pretty Face."

"Oh, and what's that?"

"I'm gonna kill the man who caused my sister's death, finally and for good."

Drake came running and strained to get past her, but Lorelai held out a booted foot and shook her head. "He's baiting you."

"It worked."

She took in a breath, the cold air piercing her eyes and making them water. Her nose felt like a frozen Popsicle and her cheeks weren't far behind.

"Gleason, you can't keep hiding out on this ranch. You're a fugitive and you will be sent to jail for killing two men now. You won't see the light of day if you kill again."

"I don't care," he shouted, adding a few more shots to show he meant business. "I'm going to do what I need to do."

Drake called out, "Booker, you should have kept going. You messed up coming back here and you know it. I don't care, either, and I'm going to get you off my land, one way or another."

"Right."

Shots rang out from the window nearest them. Gleason's aim didn't impress her, but the gunfire kept them from going in after him. Lorelai went into action and tugged Drake away, then she signaled to Bixby to move to the side. "Attack."

The dog hurled into the air near the window where they'd been standing, clawing and barking enough to give Lorelai time to shoot the door handle and kick open the front door.

Then Bixby, she and Drake all hurried inside while Rex headed toward the back. Booker Gleason was nowhere in the house. A trail of blood led them to the back just in time to hear the snowmobile cranking up.

Rex lay flat on his back but sat up and shook his head. "He butted me in the stomach and knocked my gun down before I could grab him."

Drake got in a shot, which pinged off a tree about a yard from where the snowmobile passed and then Booker disappeared in a spray of snow and mud.

"We need to go after him," she called to Drake as they hurried back to the ATV. "He's injured so he can't keep this up much longer."

Drake nodded and cranked up, waving to Rex to hold on.

They took off and rounded the curve where the snowmobile tracks left a deep gash in the snow. They could hear the engine roaring farther and farther to the east. Bixby snarled and growled low.

"Hurry," Lorelai said. Then she heard Rex behind them. He passed and waved before he went off in another direction.

"I thought he'd stay behind until we signaled," she said, watching up ahead.

"My men don't stay behind for anything, especially if someone is squatting on my land." Drake pointed to the right. "He's going to try and cut Gleason off."

Lorelai nodded. "Go."

He urged the machine to go faster, but the front plow kept slowing them down. When they heard shots up ahead, Lorelai jumped off the vehicle and signaled to Bixby. They took off running in the tracks left from the snowmobiles.

She saw Rex crouching behind his big snowmobile, while bullets pinged and dinged all around him. He peeped up and took a shot. Gleason turned and headed into a small copse of trees.

Lorelai dove into a snow-covered cluster of broken trees and heavy brush across from where Gleason had turned, then put her sights on the snowmobile up ahead. She could see Gleason glancing back. At least she could verify his identification now.

The shooting stopped briefly, giving her enough time to run to Rex's machine. Without thinking, she gave Bixby the Go command and hopped on the snowmobile and took off.

"Hey," Rex called, his rifle up. "Come back."

Lorelai didn't listen. She kept her gaze on Gleason. He turned and saw her gaining on him, his gun raised. "Bixby, stay," she called to the K-9. Bixby stopped, his whole body quivering to keep up with the chase. Drake stopped, too, then jumped off his ATV.

A shot came from behind her, causing her to duck. The shot missed her by a few feet. Glancing back she saw Rex still crouched and Drake holding up his rifle as he ran to catch up with her.

He had his rifle leveled on Gleason. Motioning for her to pull over, he ran past her and kept firing until the other snowmobile swerved and took off into an open field where about a dozen bison were huddled. If any of them took a shot now, they might hit one of the big animals or worse, cause a stampede.

She thought about how Gleason would be caught in it. He'd just shoot to kill—people or animals.

Lorelai stopped, anger and disbelief making her hit her hand against the snowmobile. "What are you doing?" she shouted at Drake.

"Lost him again," Drake said, frustration hanging on his words. "Next time, I'm not announcing us. I'm going in with guns blazing."

"I had him in my sights," she shouted. "What were you thinking?"

He frowned over at her and took off his hat to run a hand through his thick hair. "I was thinking of you, Marshal. He would have killed you if you'd gotten any closer."

"I know what I'm doing," she said through gritted teeth. "I might have shot him first."

"*Might* isn't good enough to risk your life. I told you next time, I'll be taking the lead."

Lorelai let out a breath, thinking she'd messed this up all the way around. She realized Drake would keep trying to outdo her, so she'd have to play by his rules until she could find an opportunity to do what needed to be done. Giving him a glare, she looked toward the now-empty path. "I have to agree with you, whether I like it or not. We've tried things my way. Now it's time to see what more you can do to help me, Drake. We can't let him win this time."

EIGHT

Drake wasn't sure how to take her last words to him. They headed back toward the main trail. She kept glancing around as if she expected Gleason to follow them. Drake's stomach roiled each time he thought about Gleason. This area was *mako sica* for a reason. The Lakota word for *bad lands*. The badlands had their own rules in the dead of winter. Gleason knew all those rules.

When they got to the lane leading to the house, he cut the motor and turned to her. "Look, I know you want to take Gleason back to jail. I want that, too. I'm not accustomed to someone else giving me orders."

"I'm used to this kind of talk, Drake. I'm *not* used to someone who isn't a law enforcement officer telling me what I should or shouldn't do. Got it?"

He got it all right. "I told you—my ranch, my protection."

"That's not helping."

Drake shook his head. "Are you always this stubborn?"

"I'm not stubborn, I'm determined. I'm trying to respect you and your property and I don't want to wind up lost in the snow. Don't make this harder for me."

"I want to get him and you know that. How about this? I need to check my land and my livestock. Rex and I will be on the lookout for Gleason with each stop we make, one of those being to collect Charlie's remains. You go to the house and see if you can get a call in to your team. If they're as good as you seem to think, they can help us."

He watched as she percolated on his suggestion. "I do need to call in, and I'll see if Rena got through to the coroner. I also want to go back over Gleason's last known address before he decided to go on a killing spree."

"See, now we're getting somewhere. If you weren't here, I'd be looking out for Gleason while taking care of business."

"If I weren't here, you might be dead."

Drake let out a brittle chuckle. "I reckon I might at that. Just do your work and let me do some tracking on my own for a couple of hours."

She didn't look convinced but she finally nodded and signaled to Bixby. The dog hopped into the snow and lifted his nose to the ATV. "Get to it, then," she said to Drake. "I'll find my way back to the house from here."

"Don't go off the beaten path, Marshal. Promise me that."

"I'm going to get to work on a plan to catch a criminal in an unexpected snowstorm in a state I'm still getting used to, and with a man I'm still trying to understand."

"Are you talking about Gleason, or me?" Drake asked.

"Gleason, I get," she retorted. "You, I'm not so sure."

Drake gave her a tight smile, then waved her away. He had to glance back just to make sure she went in the right direction. He didn't trust the marshal to cool her engines, but he respected her and wanted to keep her safe. Right now, he and Rex could at least check a few places on their own. And with their rifles.

Lorelai shook the snow off her clothes and saw a ray of sun trying to peek through the cotton candy clouds overhead. She thought about Savannah and the sunshine that would be sparkling there even on a December day.

You chose to come here, she reminded herself. At the time, she'd wanted to get as far away from Savannah as possible so she could forget the wreck her love life had become. Coming somewhere far away had seemed like a good idea at the time. She'd tried to love Michael, but having her parents hovering because she was still single in her mid-thirties made her actions seem desperate. She thought of how her parents loved each other despite Dad's anger control issues. When she thought of her dad's service as a local police officer and how many times he'd come close to being killed, she could see why he'd become disillusioned. He'd always done his job, put himself in danger. And Lorelai had followed his lead but with a steady heart and less anger in her soul.

Now she had to wonder. What if she couldn't catch Booker Gleason? Her superiors wouldn't be happy and she certainly wouldn't be happy. If she had no purpose, what then?

She stopped at the door to the house and said a prayer for guidance. Her parents always told her to turn to the Lord when she put her life on the line. Her dad's years in law enforcement might have left him discouraged, yet he'd taught her that sense of justice. He had not approved of her choice of careers, or her moving across the country. She had to keep going to prove things to herself, not her father.

Taking a deep breath, she motioned to Bixby. "Let's get you some food and water and your favorite play toy, how about that?"

Bixby's ears stood up and his tail wagged, "Yes, please."

She had to smile. Bixby always looked on the bright side of things.

After they were inside and free of their official gear, Lorelai went into the kitchen. Rena stood by the huge damaged window and its spiderweb cracks. Now with a weak sunshine bursting through, the still-intact window shimmered like a kaleidoscope, casting rainbow colors across the big kitchen. Rena whirled and held a hand to her heart when she saw Lorelai and Bixby. Then she wiped her eyes.

Lorilai could tell she'd been crying. "Are you all right?" she asked after grabbing Bixby's supply of food to busy herself. She didn't want to stand there and act too curious.

Rena bobbed her head. "I'm fine. Just tired. I don't like having a criminal on this land."

"How well did you know Booker?" Lorelai asked. Bixby wolfed down his food, then turned to her with expectation. She slung him a chew toy—a sturdy twisted rope with a ball attached. He tackled it with glee, unaware of the tension in the room.

Rena's cool exterior went away and her hands shook as she held them together. Something about Booker terrified this tough woman.

"What do you mean?"

Lorelai blinked. "Did you know him?"

"I don't want to talk about that man." Rena started wiping the already-clean counter. "I'm sad about Charlie. The coroner can't get through. Most of the back roads are still closed."

Lorelai's radar went up. Rena had known enough to stay away from Booker. Had he done something to scare her? Maybe she witnessed the fight between Drake and him. She would have been in her early twenties back then and pregnant. She'd also been loyal to Emma and the children so, of course, she'd dislike a troublemaker like Gleason.

Lorelai didn't push it. Instead, she checked on Bixby. When she turned back to Rena, the other woman had managed to shut down her emotions.

"I'm sorry about Charlie," she said. "Drake told me you're all close. I can see how people would bond working on a ranch."

"Yes. It's hard to maintain friendships in such isolation, yet we all stay here because we love this land. Charlie had nobody, but he gave himself over to the Lord after Rex and I persuaded him to attend church with us. I know he's at peace now."

Lorelai liked knowing that. Still, Charlie didn't deserve to die last night. "I need to let Drake know the coroner hasn't come yet."

"We might have to bury Charlie ourselves," Rena replied. "We're so isolated here."

Deciding to change the subject, Lorelai walked around the kitchen. A light snow floated across the blanketed yard.

"Can I ask you about Drake's kids?"

Rena let out a sigh of relief. "That I can talk about. Susan is a senior at the University of South Dakota, majoring in marketing, and Clay is enrolled at West Point. He always wanted to serve his country."

Lorelai took the cup of coffee Rena offered her. "They sound like good kids."

"They're great. They don't talk to Drake much these days because they're both busy. He misses them but he's always been so stoic they don't have much in common with him. I've encouraged them to come home for Christmas, but who knows."

"Do they talk to you more?"

"Yes." Rena smiled and sliced a piece of what looked like banana bread for Lorelai. "We've always been close. Gerard and Clay were thick as thieves. He had planned on going to West Point, too. Drake has connections..."

Lorelai realized Rena hadn't been crying just for Charlie. "You're thinking of him today?"

"I am."

Lorelai ate the wonderful banana bread but it felt like chalk with each bite. This attack had brought up such horrible memories for both Drake and his sister. Rena had mentioned the grief hovering over this house. What about his grown children? How much trauma were they holding inside? Emma died, Gerard died, and Rena couldn't talk about any of it much. Privacy or secrets or both?

She finished her snack while Rena chatted about the weather and the soup she'd planned for dinner. Nervous chatter.

Lorelai had to stay on task. She'd come here to find a fugitive who refused to give in. This whole vibe of nosing around the family dynamics wasn't helping her catch Booker Gleason.

And yet, she felt in her soul that all the sadness around here contained something more than him wanting revenge or trying to get even. If she ever caught the man, she'd drill him with questions regarding a lot more than causing his half-sister's death. Because something dark lurked behind the scenes on this ranch. Drake had become a recluse for many reasons and Booker Gleason had come back here for more than one reason, too.

Early the next morning, Drake watched as the coroner's van took Charlie away. The roads were clear now but after doing another search yesterday, they'd lost track of Gleason. Now, he wished he could have done more for Charlie. Charlie didn't have any close family to notify. Drake would pay for a proper burial here on the ranch in the family cemetery.

Rex walked up, his hat in his hand. "I sure will miss him."

"Yeah, me, too." He looked toward the charred bunkhouse. "For now, you'll keep staying at the main house."

They'd spent most of yesterday checking on the livestock and making sure the horses were secure in the stables while Lorelai had searched around the perimeters of the house and gone back over her reports. Just before dark, they'd found signs that showed someone had been in the stable's tack room.

Lorelai had been all business yesterday afternoon.

She didn't like losing a criminal; she didn't like civilians interfering in her work, and she sure hadn't wanted him questioning her about her personal life. He wouldn't bring *that* up again, but he had a stake in this mess and he needed to clear it up. Thankfully, she'd given him some space to explore on his own. He and Rex had seen stoked fires here and there and a few empty soup cans dropped in the woods, but no sign of Gleason.

"I appreciate that," Rex replied to his offer. "It's a might lonely around here during the holidays, and since the bunkhouse is toast I don't have many choices."

They got on the ATV and made their way back to the house.

Drake hit the steering wheel with a sharp tap. "I sure thought we'd find Gleason somewhere. It's been over twenty-four hours since we last saw him."

Rex snorted and shook his head. "He has a thousand acres to hide on, Drake, and he knows how to build a fire and stay warm. He has to be bundled up—probably saved his wound from being even worse. He'll be here until first thaw at least if we can't pin him down."

Drake pulled the ATV into the last stall of the big garage, then hopped out. "Let's get some lunch. I want to go back to the bunkhouse and have a look." He gazed toward the trail. "I'm sure the local fire marshal will want to investigate and Lorelai's team should be able to get here now."

Rex adjusted his hat. "We'll have all kinds of law officers crawling all over this place before the day's out."

"Yep, I do know that," Drake replied. "We need a posse to find Gleason and end this thing, once and for all."

"It has been hanging over us for a long time," Rex replied.

Drake needed to talk to Lorelai and make sure they were on the same page. They'd compared notes last night, but everything had stalled after their one attempt to catch Gleason. She hadn't found much in the files she pulled up again but she'd dusted the tack room for prints. Rex had been in there briefly, trying to stay warm. Drake figured Gleason had hidden there at some point, too.

They'd made it to the covered deck when Lorelai came out to greet them. "I saw the coroner's van leaving. I'm so sorry."

Drake lifted his chin but didn't speak. Rex went inside.

She tugged at her wool cap. "I also wanted to let you know I finally reached West Cole. He and a couple other local K-9 officers are coming to help us."

Glad for the help, he dreaded what might come. "Thanks, I think. Not sure how I feel about them roaming around."

"You want to catch Gleason, right? Or would you rather catch him yourself and get vengeance?"

"I'd get justice," he snapped back. Then he put a hand on her arm and lowered his tone. "I told you I won't do anything to dishonor my promise to Emma and I can promise you the same—I want to see him put away for good."

"I'll hold you to that," she replied, her words barely above a whisper. "I wish we could corner him."

For a brief moment, Drake felt the pull of her trust, her need to know she could count on him.

"We'll keep at it," he replied, unwilling to admit how he also couldn't dishonor Emma by being attracted to a woman he'd only known for a few days. But then, the Marshal had probably figured that out on her own.

NINE

Two hours later, Lorelai walked up to where Drake stood giving West Cole his statement. The snow still came and went, and while the main highways were passable, West had told her the black ice would settle in again tonight and more snow would arrive. Trying to leave this isolated ranch might be difficult.

"I'm here until Gleason is caught," she'd replied, causing West to raise his eyebrows and nod. "My SUV is totaled so I'll have to depend on you or Drake giving me a ride."

"We'll bring you a vehicle when the roads improve."

West had his K-9 partner, Gus, a yellow Lab specializing in weapons detection, along with Daniel Slater, an ATF special agent who'd led the Dakota Gun Task Force, and K-9 Dakota, a Great Dane cross-trained in protection detail and evidence retrieval. The crime scene unit had been going over Loralai's SUV, the trail, the house and the burned bunkhouse. The dogs had alerted in spots, however the weather had taken care of any definitive evidence.

Drake finished up with West and turned to Lorelai after West went to his SUV to get something. "Rex had it right earlier. This place is swarming with law enforcement people."

"What did you expect?" She liked having people she could trust with her. "They know how to find fugitives, Drake. We've tried things on our own and I'm willing to try things your way now, as I told you."

His eyes narrowed. "I reckon my way didn't bring in Gleason."

"I didn't either, so that's why they're here. They specialize in certain things—finding weapons and sniffing out evidence while offering protection. They can find Gleason and the evidence he's left behind." She waved her hand in the air. "West thinks we might have to bring in drones or possible helicopters."

"That makes sense."

"Are you uncomfortable with extra help?" she asked, hoping he'd open up to her more.

"I'm sorry," he replied when her team members glanced toward them. "This has been hectic and stressful. I'm used to doing things my way."

"I realize that." Lorelai stared him down, taking in the dark circles underneath his eyes. "This situation escalated in a hurry. However, understand I have my own ways too, but I have to play by the rules or get fired. I checked in with my superior and he's wanting results. I had to convince him the locals would be a big help. So either you're in or you can sit here and wait to hear what we find."

He let out a huff of a sigh. "You're right. I'm caught between needing justice and honoring my wife."

Lorelai wondered if that promise held him back, or if all the other variables here made him doubt himself. Vengeance and revenge could eat away at a person. And his regret likely only added to his need to see this through.

She had to believe his promise to Emma constantly warred with his determination to get even with Booker Gleason. Nagging doubts floated through her brain. She worked to put things together, to check all the boxes. This case wasn't so open and shut. She needed connections to make it all add up.

"Drake, we'll find him," she said, having that quote on speed dial. "I can't promise how it will go when we do catch Gleason. You have to trust me."

His eyes went dark at that. "I'm not good at trusting. Too much has gone wrong with me trusting people."

Lorelai saw the pain in his eyes. It had taken a lot of courage to tell her that. Looking him in the eye, she said, "You *can* trust me, and I hope your trust *in* me will be rewarded with that justice you want so badly."

He finally nodded. "I can't vouch for how I'll handle things when we're in the thick of it."

"Fair enough. I don't think he's worth you winding up behind bars with him, though."

He turned away, then pivoted. "Marshal, I don't think he's worth you getting killed, either."

"I'll keep that in mind," she replied, thinking they both lived on the edge. The awareness of him made her wonder about her own motives. This had gone from finding a killer to finding out the secrets this man held tight in his heart. To wanting to know more, find those secrets and help him heal.

And that had become part of the danger.

West came over and gave her a lifted-eyebrow frown. "Things okay here?"

"He's old-school. You know how it is—the cowboy way."

West lifted his chin and grinned. "But you're good at handling cowboys, right?"

"Usually. This one is different."

Thankfully, West didn't ask her to explain. "Update. Gus alerted near a heavy thicket off the trail to the bunkhouse. Found a box of shotgun shells. Gleason either planted them there for later, or he dropped the box running away. Daniel and Dakota haven't found any electronic devices, and what might have been in the bunkhouse has been destroyed. So no bugs or listening devices, but Gleason is using something to stay one step ahead of you. We'll find out what that is soon enough, I hope."

"Makes sense. He acted as if he'd been expecting me. Slashed my tires to keep me here, then blew up my vehicle to make sure of that and yet, his aim isn't too sharp."

West shook his head. "Hard to track. We'd better get to it. I'm guessing Corbin will be going along?"

"You'd better believe it," Drake said from behind them, his rifle ready. "My land, my protection."

"I see what you mean," West said to Lorelai. "Let's get on it, then."

Daniel walked up, armed and ready. "The fire marshal found an accelerant in the burned-out part of the bunkhouse. Good ole-fashioned Molotov cocktail."

West glanced toward Drake. "He probably dropped it on the floor and then started shooting, thinking he'd trap both of them in there."

Drake grunted. "Rex said they both managed to get out before he set the fire. Rex went one way and…Charlie ran toward the house, coming up the trail to warn me. Charlie died there on the trail while Gleason fired on us. Rex hid out until he could get to me."

"Interesting," West said. "Lorelai, what do you think?"

Lorelai had gone over her memories from the other night several times and now that she'd heard West voice it, she knew what had been bugging her. Giving Drake an apologetic nod, she turned to face the trail.

"I saw Drake with Charlie, tried to cover him so he could help his friend. We were under fire and Charlie died. We moved his body and took off toward the bunkhouse. It blew up after they'd already left, West. We thought Rex could still be in there, but he verified that he'd left when the shooting started. I think Gleason really didn't plan to kill them. He wanted them out so he could destroy the property. The man is carrying a shotgun and that means critical mass if the shooter aims just right. I think Charlie's death wasn't planned. The coroner can tell us more about that. If Gleason wanted to burn that building down for some reason, he tried to get Drake's men out before he threw that accelerant."

"You never discussed that theory with me," Drake said, his frown matching hers. "What are you implying, Marshal?"

"I'm not implying anything. Just making an observation based on what the fire marshal found and the weapon Gleason is using. Why didn't Gleason throw the accelerant through the window and run? Why did he get them out by shooting at them when he could have easily killed both of them at close range with a gun that does a lot of damage exiting the body?"

West motioned to one of the techs. "Check for bullet holes in the bunkhouse and look for bullets and casings in the burned-out areas." He glanced at Drake. "We might be able to find out if he aimed at humans or just the walls."

Lorelai took more notes. "I'll question Rex again, too. He shot at your kitchen window, Drake. He knows the glass in these windows is heavy-duty. He's been shooting all around us, trying to flush us out. What is he really after here?"

"You could have warned me," Drake said without answering her question. "We've been so busy trying to find Gleason we never went over every possibility. Now you think he's after something on the property, not just someone?"

"I'm still putting things together," she said. "Drake, I've had a nagging feeling from the beginning. Gleason didn't just come back to kill you. He wants something. Do you have an idea what that might be?"

Drake could feel the heat behind that question. He wasn't going to spill anything else in mixed company. Too many people had been hurt by Gleason's cruelty. Drake wouldn't contribute to anybody's grief or pain. Besides, he didn't know for sure but he had his own suspicions from the way his sister had been acting. He needed to talk to Rena but they weren't alone anymore.

"He's back and he killed two more people," he told Lorelai. "That's all I need to know."

West gazed between the two of them. Probably picking up on

the tension between them. "If there is anything that might help us, Mr. Corbin, it will benefit you, too."

Drake waved his hand at West, then stared at Lorelai, his heart full of disbelief. "I don't know what the man wants here, Marshal, other than he's come to kill me. How about I just go out to the pasture and holler for him to come and get me. That would make this a lot easier."

"Stop deflecting and cooperate," she said, her tone all business. "Drake, if you know anything that will help us capture Gleason, you'd better let me in on it. Sooner or later, I'll find out the truth about this and you know it."

Heat fueled by anger and regret burned through Drake like wildfire lapping at dry hay. "I say let's get out there and find Gleason so he can tell us what we need to hear. I got nothing." Then he called to Rex. "Stay close to the house with Rena."

Rex nodded. "I'm glad you said so."

Lorelai's green eyes glistened with skepticism. What did she think he was hiding? Or did she know something, and only wanted to hear the truth from him?

She whirled like a butterfly and hopped into an open four-wheel Jeep. Giving Drake a firm nod, she called, "Get in, cowboy."

Drake hopped in the back with her while her buddies West and Daniel got in the front, Daniel driving. The three K-9s managed to squeeze between the seats—two up front and Bixby in the back between Drake and Lorelai.

"You don't believe me," he said to her with a low growl.

Bixby sent his own low growl back, sensing a heavy discussion.

"I want to believe you, Drake. I've had my doubts all along. Not so much about you, just about this place and too many bad things happening. Rena is a strong woman but she changed once she heard Booker Gleason was back here. Yes, he's dangerous and a wanted man, but my instincts tell me this is deeply personal for her—just as it is for you."

"She's upset because a fugitive is threatening us and you're coming up with theories?"

"I am," Lorelai replied. "On that and so many other things."

"Like me hiding something?"

"Yes, like that. I want you to trust me, too, remember?"

"I guess we're at a standstill," he retorted. "Like two gunslingers about to end it all, one way or another."

"And that's why I have my doubts." She leaned in, her hand on Bixby. "If you plan to do this on your own even with my colleagues here, think again, okay?"

Drake let go of the breath he'd been holding. So that's what she'd been hinting at knowing. He'd let her think what she wanted, though, so she'd stay away from the tragic history of this place.

"I haven't tried to hide my thoughts on that subject. I've made it clear I want him gone. End of discussion."

"Agreed. For now." She looked up, facing front and center before she glanced back at him. "Please, Drake, don't do anything you'll regret, and don't force me to do something I'll regret."

He glanced at the snow-covered land. His land, handed down from generation to generation, with people living and dying to save it, leaving it to those who kept doing it all over again through the decades. "I regret a lot of things, Marshal. What's one more regret gonna matter?"

His phone rang before she could respond. "Yeah?"

"Boss, looks like he's hiding out in the old cabin by the north creek," Rex said on a weak breath. "I checked on the bison up that way and saw smoke coming from the chimney. Someone is there, and I'm guessing it's Gleason."

"On our way," Drake said. "Stay back till we get there."

He ended the call and told the others. "I don't know if we can get there in the Jeep, but we can make it on foot once we reach the fence line."

Daniel shifted gears and took off, the old Jeep jumping and groaning in protest, each bump shoving Drake toward her until they were shoulder to shoulder with Bixby sitting on the floorboard between them.

Lorelai pushed away and gave him an apprehensive glance. "This might all be over soon."

"Yeah, let's hope."

The unspoken things wrapped between them with all the power of a mountain mist. Drake had always been a private man. This woman—this US marshal—made him want to pour out his angst and torment. Lorelai's eyes held a light that seemed to bring life to the gray fog hanging over him and his land.

Drake wasn't sure how to handle these raw feelings right now. This had to be coming from a deep place. Gleason showing up here on a shooting spree after all these years had brought all of Drake's emotions to the surface. He would do what he'd always done in such cases. He'd walk away and never look back. That's what reclusive people did, he told himself.

Being so close to her made him think about other things he'd long ago put out of his mind. Things such as love and a true family again, which made US Marshal Lorelai Danvers a danger to him and his battered heart.

TEN

Lorelai crouched behind a jutting rock, her eyes on the small cabin leaning out between two cold-faced rock formations in a way that made her think one push would topple it over into the small valley about twenty feet below. They'd hidden the Jeep and slipped a few yards through the trees to spread out. Gleason had made a move to this cabin.

A few feet away from her, West stared through the scope of a high-powered rifle, trying to get a bead on the suspect. Daniel hovered behind an old tree trunk and talked through the radio, getting information from the crime scene techs who were now at the empty house Gleason had been hiding in earlier.

"Same bullets, same casings," he confirmed. "We're bagging whatever we can find for fingerprints. He messed up the kitchen. Found blood splatter and a dirty towel next to a bottle of alcohol. We think the wound is a through and through."

Lorelai listened to the radio chatter. "That would explain why he's still alive."

"I'll keep you posted," Daniel replied through the static.

Lorelai signed off and watched the cabin. "No movement. Think he knows we have him surrounded?"

Drake grunted from two feet over. "If he's in there and we're pretty sure he is, he'll drag this out until dark and we'll have a tough time getting back to the main house. More snow is coming overnight."

"So it's now or never," Lorelai said, gritting her teeth against the cold and her own failure. "I say we go in."

"Give it a few more minutes," West said. "I'll send Daniel and Dakota around back."

He radioed Daniel and they watched as Daniel and Dakota did a beeline into the trees and took a strenuous, slow approach to the back of the cabin. A few intense minutes seemed like hours to Lorelai.

Daniel's winded words crackled through her earbuds. "Nobody inside the cabin. Just a fire burning in the old fireplace. A fire that has to be fresh from the way it's roaring. This place might have burned down if we hadn't found it."

Lorelai's gaze met Drake's surprised eyes. "A set up way out here? What's he trying to prove now?"

Drake hit the tree branch in front of him. "He deliberately started that chimney fire to distract us, so he could go back to the house." He sprung up and headed toward the Jeep, then got in the driver's seat and cranked the engine. "We have to get back to the house. If your theory is right…he could be going after Rena."

Lorelai hid her shock, then went into action running behind him to hop in, Bixby with her. "West, check the cabin with Daniel and see if your partners alert on anything." She glanced at Drake. "What's going on?"

"No time," Drake said, popping the gears. He pulled out his phone and handed it to Lorelai. "Call Rex."

She found Rex's name and hit Call. "He's not answering."

Drake pushed the Jeep over bumps and dips. Lorelai prayed for their safety while she held on for dear life.

Once they were on the trail toward the main house, she turned and shouted low to Drake. "Why would he go after Rena, Drake?"

Drake glanced at her, shaking his head. "I don't know for sure, but what if something happened back then that Rena's not telling me?"

Shock jolted through Lorelai. "Is that what you've been hiding?"

"I'm not hiding anything, but it makes sense now," he said. "Let me get to my house, okay?"

"He's here for Rena," Lorelai said. "Why didn't tell me that?"

"I didn't know." Drake gave her a tight stare and shook his head. "If it's true, I have to get to my sister first and we'll get the details later." Then he gave her a direct stare. "I honestly don't know the truth."

Another piece of the puzzle zinged through her head like an arrow on fire. Rena's obvious fears regarding Gleason being here again, Drake's back-and-forth with his conscience eating away because he wanted Gleason dead. The secretive glances, the pallor hanging over this place.

And Rena telling her Gerard's father had died serving his country.

A rogue thought came into Lorelai's head. Danny had died on a mission. Had she found out about her pregnancy after he died? Lorelai remembered what she'd been unable to grasp after she'd been hit in the head. *Gerard had just turned sixteen when he died three years ago.* After a full-term pregnancy that meant he would have been nineteen by now if he'd lived.

Emma died twenty years ago. Rena moved in twenty years ago.

What if Danny wasn't really Gerard's father?

What if Rena and Booker had a secret past?

They made it back to the house in record time. Lorelai didn't mention her speculations to Drake. No time right now and she could be completely wrong, after all.

Drake jumped out of the Jeep and hurried to the back door, Lorelai and Bixby right behind him.

"Locked," he shouted, searching for a key on the chain he had attached to his belt. He hit the security code box after trying to open the door. "It's either dismantled or he wedged something to keep it locked."

"Did he come back for Rena?" Lorelai asked again.

"I think so," Drake said, moving from door to door. "He's managed to mess with the security system."

Lorelai didn't question him again. Instead, she radioed West and Daniel. "Suspect possibly locked in the main house and he might have two hostages. Call for more backup. Get a chopper out here."

When they heard a groan near the garage, they ran to find Rex lying there. "I was making rounds. Hit from behind."

Drake glanced all around. "Where's Rena?"

"In there with him," Rex said. "Go."

Lorelai thought she understood now. Booker and Rena must have had a relationship. Gerard could have very well been Booker's son. Did Booker find that out too late, or had he known it when he left? Had he come back for his son only to find out he was dead?

Too many questions, too many scenarios. And right now, she had to get inside this house to help Rena. Booker would use the woman as a shield to get away.

They made it around to the front, where the wide floor-to-ceiling windows should give them a view. When Drake led her to the front of the house, he let out a grunt. "He's closed the blinds. This isn't good."

"No, it isn't," Lorelai said, moving toward the front door. Bixby growled low, turning his head back toward her. Meaning he knew the culprit was nearby.

Drake's phone rang. He glanced at the number. "It's Rena."

Clicking on the call, he asked, "Are you okay?"

Drake's face went pale as he listened. Lorelai came close so she could hear.

"Hello, Drake. Long time no see."

Booker Gleason.

Drake closed his eyes and then opened them again. "Booker, what do you want?"

"You know what I want. I want the life you took away from me. I came back after I finally found out the truth."

"Take me," Drake shouted into the phone. "I'm the one you want so open the door to me and let Rena go."

"Nope. If she goes anywhere, she'll be with me, understand. I didn't go to all this trouble to lose her again."

"She wasn't ever yours to have," Drake said. "Let me see if I'm guessing right—you did what you always do—took what you wanted—and then left her alone and afraid. You open that door and be a man for once. Take me instead."

Lorelai searched Drake's face. His eyes held shock and confusion and a hovering rage. If what he'd said had happened, Booker Gleason would also go down for assaulting Rena.

And he could possibly be Gerard's father.

It all made sense now. Lorelai had to grit her teeth against the horror Rena must be going through.

"He's right," she said into the phone. "You need to surrender. Don't hurt Rena. Just come on out."

"I plan to deal with both of you later," the voice said, echoing loudly and full of anger. "I'm gonna burn this place to the ground with you and your new girlfriend inside, just as I'd planned. I wanted to burn everything here, but I need to find my son's birth certificate. I need something, anything that proves he was mine and that you and Rena owe me, big-time."

"What?" Drake rushed forward. "You are a sick man, Gleason. You don't care about that boy or what you did. You just want an easy way out."

Lorelai grabbed Drake's arm to stop whatever he had in mind. "Let me talk to him."

"It won't do any good," Drake said so they could both hear him. "Booker, take me. Burn me down with the house because you won't get any money from my family. Let Rena go. You've hurt her enough."

Lorelai had a sick feeling inside her stomach. She detested men who used women and left them broken and damaged. Booker had attacked and taken advantage of Rena. That would explain why Rena had been so upset when she heard Booker had returned.

Lorelai leaned in. "Can we talk to Rena? Make sure she's okay?"

Gleason chuckled. "She's fine. She'll be even better when we get away from this place. All we need is that birth certificate. She's his mother; I'm his father. Simple."

Lorelai thought none of this was simple. "You'll take Rena, force us inside and what—set the place on fire, hoping you can come back and claim ownership. What about Drake's children?"

"I'll take care of them soon enough. They should be on their way here. I had Rena send them an important message."

Drake pivoted away from Lorelai and headed for the porch. "Let me in there, Gleason. You've made a fatal mistake."

Lorelai ran behind him, Bixby on her heels. "Drake, no. Think of Rena right now."

He stopped and leaned over, his breath heaving. "I can't let him hurt anyone else. I have to know Rena and my kids are safe."

Lorelai took his phone. "Let me talk to her," she shouted to Gleason. "You're surrounded and we have more law enforcement on the way."

Rex came hobbling around the house, but Lorelai motioned for him to stay away from the porch.

Booker spoke again. "Bring it, Marshal. I've got nothing to lose and you know that makes a man dangerous."

Drake took the phone back, his voice rising with each word. "Gleason, if you don't bring Rena out to me now, I'll find you and get this over with, something I should have done long ago."

The line went dead.

Rex sank down on the steps, his head in his hand.

Drake turned to Lorelai and she saw the anger running through him like rock fissures as he shook his head and looked down at the ground. "He did this. He abused Rena and left her. She got pregnant and I assumed Danny was the father." Drake stabbed his fingers against a nearby post. "If I'd known for certain—"

"You would have killed him," Lorelai said. "That's why she never told you, Drake."

"I wish she had. I just wish she had."

Lorelai swallowed the bile rising in her throat. "He thinks Gerard was his son. And he admitted he found out the truth. Did you know this already?"

Drake shook his head. "I didn't know. The day Gerard died I got suspicious. She said things that didn't make sense. Blamed herself for Gerard's death."

"And the drunk driver, Drake?"

Drake's dark eyes went misty with tears. "I can't be sure because it was a hit-and-run. Now I think the driver is the man holding Rena hostage."

She couldn't ask him anything more. Instead, Lorelai sank down with Drake on the front steps and held him in her arms. Rex moved toward them and stared up at the house.

Finally, she whispered, "I'm going to find a way into that house."

Drake didn't speak for a moment, then he lifted his head. "There's a secret door into the basement. I built it for the kids when they were little. Honestly, I always told them to hide there if anybody came messing with us. I can't fit in it but—"

"I can," Lorelai said, lifting up like a rocket. "And so can Bixby. Show me where it is and where it leads. Now."

ELEVEN

Drake led her around the side of the house, careful to stay away from the windows. They'd left Rex watching the front then scaled the narrow areas between the shrubbery and the stone walls to get to the open space underneath the upper deck, Bixby remaining quiet as he followed. Drake knocked down the snow piled up around the deck beams and motioned to Lorelai. They dipped down to get away from the wind and the slippery mush. The deck overhead held a foot of snow, giving them more protection.

Huddling there, Drake pointed to the foundation. "The door is about three-feet high and maybe a foot or so wide. It's behind this storage area," he told her, whispering as he lifted his hand toward the higher elevation of the house. The snow didn't reach all the way underneath. "You'll need to get past some flowerpots and corn-toss boards. I can help."

"No, see if you can get in any other way," she replied. "Don't let them know you're there. He'll shoot you and possibly your sister if he sees you or Rex."

"Got it."

"Where does the secret door lead?"

"Into the laundry room in the basement," he said. "There's a big screen underneath the folding counter. Slip that off and you can wiggle through and look for a small staircase on the other side of the hallway from the kitchen. Near Rex's bedroom. I put the opening there because it's across from the back door and the garage."

"So they'd crawl through and run out the back stairs?"

"Exactly. They played in it until they got too old and lost interest. I haven't thought about it in years."

"Okay," she said, glancing around. "I'll get in and try to find where he's got Rena. Bixby knows the drill. Don't do anything unless you have no other choice. West and Daniel should be here soon. I'm going to warn them to stay quiet and wait, okay."

He nodded. "Marshal, you don't need to do this."

"Yes, I do, Drake. I'll be okay, hear me?"

"You can't promise that."

"If I don't try to get in there, Rena could die or worse, be taken on the run as a hostage."

He swallowed, his gaze marbled with pain, his eyes dark as a black night. Putting his hands on her puffer jacket, he leaned over, his world-weary face peppered with doubt and hope. "Watch your back, Marshal."

"I will."

With that, he crouched as he scooted toward the yard.

Lorelai took a breath and radioed West to give him an update. "Come to the house and wait for my cue. This is a volatile situation."

She signed off and started moving things, her mind whirling between the look on Drake's face when he'd left and Rena being a victim who had to stay quiet to protect her son.

Those questions had been answered. Booker had come back thinking he could cash in on their grief by proving he was the father of Rena's son, who could have inherited the ranch along with Drake's two children, same way Rena and Drake had inherited.

She found the secret door and pulled out her penlight so she could see, hoping no creepy crawlers were down here. The icy-cold tunnel gave her the shivers. She managed to shimmy inside and crawl along on her hands and knees, cold dirt scraping at her palms and her blue jeans. Bixby followed, doing a dog-crawl, his eyes wide, his ears and snout on the alert.

They moved in silence, the darkness and old spiderwebs surrounding her while she listened for any noise above. When she heard footsteps overhead to her right, Lorelai stopped and took a breath, then went still. Booker and Rena!

Straining to hear, she listened as the words grew louder.

"You never told me the truth, Rena." Gleason's voice. "I accidentally killed our son and you did nothing to stop it."

Lorelai let out a gasp and held a hand to her mouth, her heart hurting for Drake's sister.

Then she heard Rena's sniffles, and a moan. "Stop it! You were drunk. I screamed at Gerard to come back after you blurted out the truth. I begged him to listen. I couldn't tell anyone, Booker. What you did, how you treated me, made me so ashamed. Drugging my drink and taking advantage of my grief. I'll never understand how you found out about Gerard. I never wanted you to know. I never wanted him to know."

The confession seared a path in Lorelai's brain. Booker wouldn't get away with this. Rena had told the story, maybe in hopes her brother or Lorelai could hear her. Smart woman.

"I came back that day all those years ago to see you, to try and make amends. It had been a while, and I had a job and everything," Gleason went on. "We could have been together."

"You shouldn't have come here at all."

"No, I had every right to be here to see you. But imagine me walking up to the porch only to see a younger version of myself—my son."

"He was never yours."

Lorelai heard a banging, like a hand hitting a wall. "My son—don't deny it. A reason to live and it's your fault he's not here today because you kept that from both of us."

Rena didn't respond to his accusations. Lorelai started to move again. Then she heard crying, sobs so full of anguish she could feel them down to her soul.

Rena.

Taking off again, Lorelai knew she had to get Rena out of there. The woman would take care of things on her own and that wouldn't help anyone. She and Bixby had to hurry.

Drake roamed around the outside perimeters of the house, thinking he should have gone in after Booker. He had two strong women to think about. He didn't want either of them to get caught in the crossfire.

When he heard a motor roaring out on the trail, he saw Rex waving to West and Daniel. The two officers and their K-9s hopped off the four-wheeler and rushed through the mushy snow to where Drake stood.

"Hold back," he said. "Lorelai is going inside."

"How?" West asked, glancing around.

"A tunnel I made for my kids when they were little. It's walled with wood and safe. Has an escape screen in the laundry room just below the kitchen. She should be there by now."

Daniel shook his head, looking concerned for his agent.

"I couldn't fit," Drake said. "She offered. And frankly, I couldn't stop her."

"He brings up a good point," West said. "What's next, cowboy?"

Drake ignored the tease. "She said to wait. I'm not good at waiting."

"Chopper's on the way," Daniel reported, glancing at the distant hills. "Meantime, we're here and we're ready."

"We have four of us," West replied. "We'll surround the house. Two up front and two here in the back."

"Okay." Drake stared them all down. "If she's not out with my sister in fifteen minutes, I'm going in."

"I'll be right behind you," Rex said in a definitive tone.

"We'll all go in if he doesn't come out." West moved toward Drake. "You and me up front and Rex and Daniel back here. A dog with both."

"I can live with that," Drake said, already crouching as he moved toward the front of the long rectangular house.

"You got it, boss," Rex said, lifting his chin to Daniel.

They split up and found their spots, the officers with their K-9s.

Drake shimmied with anger and impatience as he sat crouched behind a holly bush near the long front porch. His mind went to dark places and then back to prayer. Sweat trickled down his backbone with a spiderweb grip and his head hurt like a firecracker had exploded inside.

How would he ever forgive himself and get over this hatred he felt toward Booker Gleason? If something happened to his sister or Lorelai, it would be the same nightmare all over again.

Across from where he hid, West Cole watched the house and Drake, his K-9 ready for some action. The officers didn't trust Drake and he couldn't blame them. Now that he knew the whole truth and his worst assumptions had turned out to be correct, he felt sick inside. Booker had ruined more than one life, and Drake hadn't moved beyond his own grief to see that.

Lorelai went in there to save his sister while he sat here like a duck by the water. He had to do something and soon.

Lorelai put her hands on the white mess screen in the laundry room and listened for any more shouting. The house had grown eerily quiet. The sun would be setting soon and night would come.

She lifted the screen and silently laid it to the side underneath the long counter. Two big storage cabinets were built on each side with the middle just wide enough for her to squeeze through. A good idea and one that might save them.

She unfurled herself and stood, checking her gun and her vest. Ready. Then she turned to Bixby and gave him the silent command.

She reached for the door when she heard a scream and then gunfire.

Hurling the door back against the wall, she rushed up the four steps to the hallway and into the kitchen. No one.

Then she went through the open space leading to the den. Empty.

On her way upstairs, she heard a rustle in the bedroom across from the kitchen. Motioning to Bixby to come, Lorelai hugged the hallway walls until she'd made it back to the closed bedroom door.

Rena screamed, "Let me go!"

Lorelai kicked the door open and rushed in, her gun aimed. Motioning to Bixby, she gave the search alert.

Bixby stopped short for an instant before he turned and growled. Rena stood in the middle of the room, one hand to her mouth. "I'm sorry, Lorelai," she whispered.

Gleason stood behind her, a gun against Rena's ribs.

Lorelai glanced around just as Gleason tossed Rena to the floor and charged at Lorelai, knocking her off her feet. Her gun went flying one way and she went the other, just missing a sturdy wooden chair arm, Bixby's angry barks echoing behind her.

"Guard," she managed to call out. Bixby had to protect Rena.

She flipped, grasping at the floor as she searched for her weapon. Gleason grabbed her by her coat and threw her back onto the carpet. He leaned over her, his eyes glazed with anger and hate, his face scarred and scratched, a dirty strand of dark hair plastered across his forehead.

"You won't get away from me this time, Marshal. I could have had this over and done if you hadn't shown up."

Lorelai kicked at him. She needed Bixby now. "No, you won't get away from me, Gleason." Searching for Bixby, she saw him near where Rena stood frozen. "Bixby, attack."

The K-9 leaped against Gleason's back. Gleason pushed him off. He slapped Lorelai, jarring her to the point of seeing stars, his grimy hands grabbing at her neck. Lorelai tried to tell Rena to run, but she couldn't breathe, couldn't speak. She saw more stars and felt a blackness taking over, Bixby's barks and snarls screaming through her head. Trying once more to kick up and flip him away, she used all her strength in one last effort. Gleason held on, shouting profanity as Bixby attacked him from behind.

Lorelai managed to grab his arms and fight back. She couldn't find air. As her body gave up the fight, she tried to see Rena, tried to get free.

A shot rang out and Gleason jerked up with a loud groan, then fell away from her. Lorelai inhaled and took in air, then coughed, her throat throbbing with agony. Bixby stood over Gleason, snarling.

The room went silent for a moment and then humans and dogs rushed in, taking over. Strong arms lifted Lorelai and held her close.

Drake.

"You're okay," he kept whispering. "You're okay."

Lorelai nodded, tried to speak. "I'm...fine."

Drake kissed her on the forehead. "Thank you, Marshal."

Then West came over, and Drake said, "Take care of her. I have to see to my sister."

West helped Lorelai sit up. Still shaking and coughing, she saw Rena sitting on the bed, Lorelai's gun in her hand.

Lorelai gasped. "Rena?"

"She shot him," Drake replied. "My sister saved your life."

Drake sat next to her, his arm on his sister's shoulder. Rex saw them and hurried to her other side. Booker Gleason lay there dead, blood pooling around him, his eyes wide open and gazing into nothing.

"It's over," Drake said, refusing to let go of his silent sister. "It's over."

Lorelai managed to stand and make it to the bed. Rex stood so she could sit next to Rena. In a hoarse whisper she asked, "Rena, are you okay?"

Rena turned, her expression blank, her skin pale. "Yes, finally, it's over."

Bixby nudged Lorelai's leg, then studied Rena before he laid his head against Rena's lap.

And that's when Rena started sobbing.

Christmas Eve

Drake stood at the apartment door wondering why he'd come here. His sister and his children had forced his hand and told him he needed to invite US Marshal Lorelai Danvers to spend Christmas with them.

"Don't come back without that woman," Rena had said, her voice and her gumption both strong again and Rex by her side, grinning.

Drake's confusion and apprehension made him whirl to leave her place, but the door opened and there stood Lorelai in a cute red Christmas sweatshirt that featured a dog with a Santa hat on his head, and flannel pants with reindeers dancing across them.

"I didn't even knock," he said, his heart betraying him with heavy beats.

Bixby moved into view. "Aw, the dog alerted you, right?"

"It's what he does," she said, motioning Drake in with a sweep of her hand.

Drake entered and took in the modern townhouse. A bright and functional kitchen in one corner and a cozy little den across from a small fireplace made the place welcoming. A tiny Christmas tree decorated with white lights held beachy ornaments along with snowmen.

"Nice," he said, taking off his coat and hat.

"What are you doing here?" she asked, her arms wrapped against her stomach in a protective mode. Did she have the jitters same as him?

"My family told me to come and get you and Bixby and bring you to the ranch for Christmas."

Her expression changed from all business to a soft-glowing realization that presented a tight smile. "Really?"

"Really," he said. "Wasn't sure but they didn't have to push me too hard to get here."

The glow went out. "I wouldn't dream of imposing."

Bixby grunted, his gaze moving between them, waiting for some action.

Drake chuckled and pulled Lorelai into his arms. "You are definitely an imposition, Marshal, but I sure miss you."

"I—"

He didn't give her time to argue. Tuning his head out, he let his heart do the talking. Drake held her closer, then kissed her—a good long kiss that spoke much better than he could. Finally, he leaned back and said, "Let me rephrase that. *I* want *you* to spend Christmas with me and my family."

Bixby's interest in this situation increased. He let out a low yelp.

Lorelai tried to speak but Drake put his finger on her lips. "Say yes."

She glared at him, then she bobbed her head. "Yes."

"Okay then, grab some gear and let's go."

"Wait? How is Rena? How are your children? How are you?"

"Rena is doing good. She'd going to a counselor here in Plains City and she and Rex are talking marriage later. She's a strong woman. She'll grieve forever, but she won't live in fear."

Lorelai nodded at that. "She went through so much and held it all so close to her heart. I'm happy for her and Rex. He's a true hero."

Drake lowered his head. "We both held our cards too close to our chest and you saved us, Lorelai. Now Susan and Clay have heard all about the amazing Lorelai Danvers and her superhero partner, Mr. Bixby."

Bixby's ears went up and he gave Drake a doggy smile.

"And how are you? I mean, you did your part, too, but I hope you're handling your own guilt about not knowing the truth. That must be hard to deal with."

Drake nodded then touched a finger to her hair. "Right now,

I'm fine. Gleason is gone and my family can finally heal. You and I met under bad circumstances and the adrenaline rush has cooled down. I'd like to get to know you better if you don't mind."

"I'd like that, too. But, Drake, what about…your wife?"

A mist hit Drake in the eye. He swallowed, accepting that deep piercing moving through his heart. "My kids think Emma would be happy for me. For us. If we work it out, of course."

"I'd like to believe that," she replied, relief softening her gaze. "I reckon we'll just see how it goes."

One Year Later, Christmas Day

Lorelai stood looking out the window over the snow, remembering all the horrible things she'd witnessed here that had now been surpassed by all the good things happening. Last Christmas, right after they'd seen justice served, she'd enjoyed being with Drake and his family and having a quiet celebration with them. Now, a year later, she was still hanging around and she was in love with a man her dad approved of completely.

Tonight, this house sparkled with brightness, and everyone laughed and enjoyed sugar cookies and chocolate cake. Bixby lay curled up by the fire, his dark eyes taking it all in.

Drake came up to her, offering a cup of hot chocolate. "So what do you think, Marshal? We made it through this year without even a scratch."

She turned to him, her heart open and willing. "We'll have some tough times—such as when I have to go out and do my job and you'll worry and give me advice and ask me not to go."

"Okay, yeah, but—"

"But, Drake Corbin, I'll always return because I'll want to see you and Rena and Rex and the bison and Susan and Clay. In spite of everything, I like it here."

"And I like having you here." He set her mug on a nearby

table, then wrapped his arms around her. "Plus, I've still never been to Savannah."

"I'll take you there," she whispered before they kissed.

"Maybe for our honeymoon."

"You haven't proposed yet. Slow, remember?"

"I'm an impatient man. Besides, I made a wish on that gold star." He pointed to the big tree. "Maybe we'll talk about how much we love each other and maybe you'll agree to marry me?"

She yanked his head down and kissed him again. "Maybe that can happen, after all."

Applause pulled them apart. They laughed and sat down by the Christmas tree while the silent night surrounded them and the joy of Christmas bonded them with a sweet promise of hope. Tonight, the snow didn't look so treacherous.

* * * * *

If you enjoyed Lorelai's story, don't miss the rest of the Dakota K-9 Unit series!

Chasing a Kidnapper
by Laura Scott, April 2025

Deadly Badlands Pursuit
by Sharee Stover, May 2025

Standing Watch
by Terri Reed, June 2025

Cold Case Peril
by Maggie K. Black, July 2025

Tracing Killer Evidence
by Jodie Bailey, August 2025

Threat of Revenge
by Jessica R. Patch, September 2025

Double Protection Duty
by Sharon Dunn, October 2025

Final Showdown
by Valerie Hansen, November 2025

Christmas K-9 Patrol
by Lynette Eason and Lenora Worth, December 2025

*Available only from Love Inspired Suspense.
Discover more at LoveInspired.com.*

Dear Reader,

Thank you for coming along to be snowed in with Lorelai, Bixby and Drake. Lorelai showed up to find a fugitive and she did. But she also realized why she'd moved across the country. She decided she needed to stop running after she met Drake.

Drake had shuttered himself on his land and refused to let go of his grief and his pledge to his wife to be a better man. He wrestled with that decision until the past showed up and made him come to terms with all his grief and mistakes.

These two wounded people came together in the worst of circumstances, but they survived the storm. I hope that whatever you are dealing with today, you can overcome your circumstances and find your way back to hope and love. Sending you a big hug and I hope you enjoyed this story.

Until next time, may the angels watch over you.

Always,
Lenora

Get up to 4 Free Books!

We'll send you 2 free books from each series you try PLUS a free Mystery Gift.

Both the **Love Inspired®** and **Love Inspired® Suspense** series feature compelling novels filled with inspirational romance, faith, forgiveness and hope.

YES! Please send me 2 FREE novels from the Love Inspired or Love Inspired Suspense series and my FREE gift (gift is worth about $10 retail). After receiving them, if I don't wish to receive any more books, I can return the shipping statement marked "cancel." If I don't cancel, I will receive 6 brand-new Love Inspired Larger-Print books or Love Inspired Suspense Larger-Print books every month and be billed just $7.19 each in the U.S. or $7.99 each in Canada. That is a savings of 20% off the cover price. It's quite a bargain! Shipping and handling is just 50¢ per book in the U.S. and $1.25 per book in Canada.* I understand that accepting the 2 free books and gift places me under no obligation to buy anything. I can always return a shipment and cancel at any time by calling the number below. The free books and gift are mine to keep no matter what I decide.

Choose one:
- ☐ **Love Inspired Larger-Print** (122/322 BPA G36Y)
- ☐ **Love Inspired Suspense Larger-Print** (107/307 BPA G36Y)
- ☐ **Or Try Both!** (122/322 & 107/307 BPA G36Z)

Name (please print)

Address   Apt. #

City   State/Province   Zip/Postal Code

Email: Please check this box ☐ if you would like to receive newsletters and promotional emails from Harlequin Enterprises ULC and its affiliates. You can unsubscribe anytime.

Mail to the Harlequin Reader Service:
IN U.S.A.: P.O. Box 1341, Buffalo, NY 14240-8531
IN CANADA: P.O. Box 603, Fort Erie, Ontario L2A 5X3

Want to explore our other series or interested in ebooks? Visit www.ReaderService.com or call 1-800-873-8635.

---

*Terms and prices subject to change without notice. Prices do not include sales taxes, which will be charged (if applicable) based on your state or country of residence. Canadian residents will be charged applicable taxes. Offer not valid in Quebec. This offer is limited to one order per household. Books received may not be as shown. Not valid for current subscribers to the Love Inspired or Love Inspired Suspense series. All orders subject to approval. Credit or debit balances in a customer's account(s) may be offset by any other outstanding balance owed by or to the customer. Please allow 4 to 6 weeks for delivery. Offer available while quantities last.

Your Privacy—Your information is being collected by Harlequin Enterprises ULC, operating as Harlequin Reader Service. For a complete summary of the information we collect, how we use this information and to whom it is disclosed, please visit our privacy notice located at https://corporate.harlequin.com/privacy-notice. Notice to California Residents – Under California law, you have specific rights to control and access your data. For more information on these rights and how to exercise them, visit https://corporate.harlequin.com/california-privacy. For additional information for residents of other U.S. states that provide their residents with certain rights with respect to personal data, visit https://corporate.harlequin.com/other-state-residents-privacy-rights/.

LIRLIS25